CHEATING
SAVED MY  Marriage

WOMEN DO IT BETTER

ArLancia Williams

For permission requests, write to the publisher, addressed "Attention: Permissions Coordinator," 205 N. Michigan Avenue, Suite #810, Chicago, IL 60601. 13th & Joan books may be purchased for educational, business or sales promotional use. For information, please email the Sales Department at sales@13thandjoan.com.

Printed in the U. S. A.

First Printing, November 2023

Library of Congress Cataloging-in-Publication Data has been applied for.

ISBN: 978-1-961863-17-0

I would like to thank my husband Antawan,
for supporting me in everything I do. Antawan
has grown to be an amazing husband. He put
his personal beliefs and pride on the sideline
and stood beside me as I wrote this novel.
He is and always will be my best friend.

I would like to thank my biggest cheerleader,
my youngest daughter Miani, who is always
supportive and shows up for her mom.

I would like to thank my aunt, Teresa,
for always listening to my ideas.

Lastly I would like to thank all of my readers
that took the time to pick up this book and
give my words a chance. I hope that you find
my book funny, hopeful and it gives you
the courage to fight for your marriage.

Prologue

Mike can't believe he's here. He's an attractive, 6 foot 3 tall, eight figure earning real estate professional black man and he's sitting in front of Dr. Phil curled in the fetal position with the glory tear falling down his face.

Dr. Phil sits in his plaid jacket, blue shirt and tan slacks with a legal pad sitting on his crossed legs. He stares at Mike with a blank face as Mike rocks back and forth. Finally Mike speaks.

"I know, I know. I know what I did was wrong but she wasn't supposed to get a nigga back like that." Dr. Phil's eyebrow raises.

"Do you normally quote Jay-Z?"

Mike quickly sits up with an impressed look on his face as he wipes his eyes.

"Jay-Z is a genius. I learned everything I know from him. Well, him and the godfather Kevin Samuels."

Dr. Phil writes the word, interesting, on the notepad. Mike leans over trying to see what he's writing.

"What?"

"I find it interesting that a man in your current predicament is influenced by a polarizing social media influencer and a documented adulterer."

"Are you judging me, Doc?"

"It's kinda my job."

Mike leaps to his feet, pacing around the office. He talks under his breath.

"See! This is why black people don't go to therapy. I knew I shoulda got a black therapist."

"I hear Dr. Umar is available." Dr. Phil snaps back.

Mike stops pacing, he looks at Dr. Phil with a stern face.

"Now is not the time for jokes."

"Who's joking?"

Mike and Dr. Phil engage in a Mexican stare off with each other for what seems like forever. Eventually, Dr. Phil exhales in an attempt to calm Mike down.

"Why don't you just start at the beginning. What events led up to you being here with me today?"

Mike flops down in the gray suede armchair. Claps his hands as he leans forward.

"Well, in the beginning everything was Gucci—"

Chapter 1

Mia, a beautiful 30-year-old, natural long haired black woman, snatches open the drawer of a beautiful cherry wood dresser, chipping one of her well-manicured French tipped nails, but she doesn't care. She violently throws designer garments into her Louis Vuitton leather duffle bag while she ignores Mike's pleas.

He stands behind her, shirtless with the bottom half of his body wrapped in a bed sheet. He has the look of fear and embarrassment on his face, like a teenage boy who's been caught having sex with a girl in his mother's bed. He doesn't know whether to keep his distance or approach Mia.

To add insult to injury, there's a frantic naked woman searching around the room for her clothes. She doesn't take her eyes off Mia, which is hindering her from finding her clothes. Finally, Mike speaks, stammering over his words.

"Mia, baby, com'on, please. It's not even like that."

The naked woman stops her search, looks at Mia. She talks in between labored breaths. She nervously nods her head up and down.

"Yeah! Yeah! It's not like that."

Mia tosses the duffle bag on the floor, hard. She turns around looking at Mike and the naked woman with tears and fire in her eyes. Mia can't believe the audacity of Mike. Talking as if this is the only time he's done this. It's not like what? Not like he just had his dick in some pussy that was probably washed in a gas station sink before she came over here.

Despite how she felt on the inside, Mia is not ready to leave Mike. Truthfully, she isn't sure if she ever will. So instead of giving Mike all the smoke, she dials it down a little.

"That's what you said the last time and the time before that all the way to the first time. You must take me for a goddamn fool."

"Girl, he fooled us both."

Mia glares at the woman as if she's about to snatch off her lace front. The woman hides behind Mike, nearly tripping over her jeans.

"You're right Mia, I shouldn't be saying anything. I'm not gonna make any sudden moves, I'm just gonna bend down slowly and pick up my jeans. And as soon as I find my panties, I'm outta here. OK?"

The woman drops down to the floor, grabs her jeans and struggles to put them on quickly.

Mike slumps his shoulders. He looks at Mia with remorse and tenderness in his eyes. He struggles to walk toward her due to the sheet being tightly wrapped around his legs.

Mia rolls her eyes as he reaches her then looks away from him knowing the bullshit that is about to come out of his mouth. Mike looks down at the open bag then he looks back at Mia. He talks in a softened tone trying to lessen Mia's anger.

"You just gonna leave after all we've been through?" Mia chuckles as she can't believe Mike is trying to make himself out to be the victim in this situation. *Typical nigga-ish* she thought to herself.

"You mean after everything you put ME through!" Mia yells back. Her voice is so loud that Mike jumps and the naked woman hits her head while looking under the bed for her shoes. Mike and Mia stare at each other quietly. Mia sucks her teeth, bends down to pick up the bag but Mike snatches it out of her hands.

"I love you."

Mia rolls her eyes, exhales with disbelief. The naked woman pops from under the bed holding up her shoe proudly proclaiming she found this first of her shoes. Mike and Mia ignore her as they continue talking.

"This? This ain't love Mike! Clearly I'm not what you want so I'm not going to stand in your way of being happy. I know my worth. It's about time I find a man that knows it too."

Mia says with tears in her eyes. She snatches the bag from Mike, zips it then throws it over her shoulder. She looks at him tenderly with tears streaming down her face.

"Goodbye Mike."

Mia pushes past Mike as she storms toward the door. Mike breathes heavily. His eyes widen and search around the room frantically. He's trying his best to think about what he can do or say to stop Mia from leaving. Everything seems to move in slow motion for Mike. Each step Mia takes to the door matches his heartbeat. He sweats, trembles and sways side to side. Mike drops to one knee and belts out, "Mia! Will you marry me?"

Mia stops dead in her tracks. She lets out a surprised gasp. She grabs her chest and closes her eyes. The woman stands up looking shocked with her other shoe in hand. She smiles genuinely at the sight of Mike on one knee.

Slowly she turns around. She sees Mike holding a ring box in the air. Mia lets the duffle bag drop to the floor. She slowly walks toward Mike, not taking her eyes off the ring. She extends her left hand allowing Mike to slide the ring on her finger. She smiles big.

"Yes! What took you so long?"

Mike stands facing Mia and the two kiss passionately. After the kiss, Mike and Mia stare into each other's eyes, both extremely happy with each other. The woman awes.

"Aww, that's sweet."

Now fully dressed, with her shirt inside out and holding her shoes close to her chest, the woman quietly tip toes toward the door. She whispers.

"Bye Mike. See you next week?"

Mia and Mike's heads snap toward the woman looking at her as if she's lost her mind. Immediately, she realizes her mistake. She adjusts her composure, holding up one hand in surrender.

"Right, right. Congrats sis. Ya'll send me an invite to the wedding."

Mike and Mia turn back to gazing at each other as the woman leaves the room. Inside, Mia feels elated and finally loved. She believes that Mike does really love her and he's chosen her, which is the only thing she's ever wanted from him. His money doesn't matter to her. The gifts and extravagant Atlanta nights out on the town fail to satisfy her. For years, Mia has loved Mike with the hopes of one day it would be enough for him to stop his cheating ways and fully commit to her. Mike's proposal is the gesture she's been waiting for.

Unfortunately for Mike, his feelings are different. He's not ready for marriage and if he's being honest with himself, he doesn't know if he wants to be married at all. Why did he propose to Mia? It's simple. He doesn't want her to be with another man. Despite his sexual indiscretions, Mike believed that Mia would always be there. He's cheated repeatedly throughout their relationship but she's never left let alone threatened to leave.

Mike bought the ring 2 years ago as a get out of jail free card. He anticipated this day coming. The day Mia would actually catch him in the act. Knowing the woman he's been with for so long, Mike knew that if Mia saw him cheating with her own two eyes, she would undoubtedly leave him. But the idea of actually getting married never crossed his mind. But now here we are.

Thoughts about how long he can go without having the actual wedding flood Mike's mind. Strangely, he felt an immense sense of anxiety and a feeling of loss as soon as Mia said yes. He asks himself, why does he feel this way? Is it marriage he doesn't want or is it marriage with Mia he doesn't want? Or does it mean the death of random pussy whenever he wants it?

One thing is for sure, Mike isn't quite ready to let Mia go. Like most men, he wants to have his cake and eat it too.

Inside a very upscale barbershop the decor looks more like a gentlemen's club than a barbershop. With the exception of the bright ring lights at every barber station, the lights are low giving the shop a warm comfortable feel. Each side of the room is decorated with large black leather barber chairs and large flat screens over each barber section. A large logo decal sits in the middle of the mahogany wood floors that matches the deep brown wood finishings throughout the rest of the shop.

Patrons wait in an area sitting on fancy sofas and armchairs. Some smoke cigars, others smoke and drink liquor from the vast bar toward the back of the space. The sounds of trap music competes with the boastful voices and laughter from the barbers and patrons.

Mike enters the barbershop dressed in jet black jeans that are tapered just enough to show off his Travis Scott retro Jordan 1 sneakers and a blinding white Gucci shirt which allows his gold cross necklace to shine brighter. Mike is immediately bombarded with a loud and inviting welcome.

He's been coming to the same barbershop for 20 years. The barbers and many of the elder men have watched him grow up from a hilarious comedic kid to the off-the-cuff, still funny man he is today. At the same time, Mike has seen the barbershop transform from a rundown 2-station shop, to the luxurious barbershop that regular men and Atlanta's elite frequent.

Despite rubbing elbows with entertainers, actors and athletes, for Mike, the shop is his home. It's his oasis, one of the last safe places for black men in a world that constantly reminds them it hates them. Additionally, it's the one place Mike can be completely honest. As he makes his way through the shop, he gives several men head nods as he makes his way to the awaiting barber chair. Mitchell, the 60-year-old heavyset barber, the only barber Mike allows to touch his hair, uses the black cape to beat the loose hair off the chair before Mike sits down.

Mitchell puts the cape around Mike's neck as he looks at Mike in the mirror. Mike sits slumped with a worried look on his face. Mitchell stops just as he's about to pick up a comb. He gives Mike an inquisitive look.

"What's wrong? Somebody step on your Jordans?" He asks as the shop erupts in laughter.

Mike exhales as he searches for the right words to say. His mind races. Should he tell the men at the shop what he did? Or should he lie and make up something else. On one side, if he does tell the men he has to deal with the jokes, snickers but even worse, the congratulations he's gonna receive. But on the other side, if he doesn't tell the men the truth, he'd be ruining the sanctity of the shop by lying.

The choice is a simple one. He has to tell them the truth, and he does. Mike blurts out, "I proposed to Mia."

Immediately Mitchell pops the back of Mike's head with the comb.

"Are you stupid? What you go and do that for?" Before Mike could answer, one of the elder men jumped to Mike's defense.

"Ahh leave that boy alone. Marriage is a beautiful thing." Mitchell fires back at the man, "Ain't nobody talkin' to you Frank. I'm talkin' to the boy."

Mitchell pops the back of Mike's head with the comb again. Mike winces at the sting. Mike turns around, firm yet playful in his response.

"I love you big bro but if you pop me again, it's gonna be a problem. Don't let ya age write a check your body can't cash."

The shop laughs, Mitchell waves them off. He spins Mike around in the chair to face him. He stares at him for a few seconds, trying to figure out if Mike is telling the truth or not. Eventually he spins Mike back around shaking his head No.

"I call cap. Ain't that what you young people say nowadays? Cap?" Mike chuckles.

Yeah, you used it correctly. But I'm deadass, I proposed to her yesterday." Mitchell looks over his glasses. "Deadass? No, I don't know that one. Why'd you do it?" Mike looks around before answering, "She caught me cheatin'. She was almost out the door. I had to do something to make her stay. She was gonna leave. What was I supposed to do?"

The men in the shop negatively react to Mike's revelation in animated comedic fashion. The shop is in complete pandemonium.

James, another barber but younger, cutting hair next to him, sucks his teeth as he cuts a man's hair. He speaks loudly to cut through the noise.

"You got to be the dumbest mofo up in here. Who proposes after gettin' caught slangin' the blicky to another broad?" Another man adds his opinion.

"Facts. She gave you a way out and you didn't even have to give up half your money. You just gave her pussy all the power. Couldn't be me."

A lot of the men agree. Mike looks at the man with his face turned up.

"I know you ain't talkin'. You couldn't find pussy on Fulton Industrial." The shop erupts in knee slapping laughter again. Mitchell has to stop cutting Mike's hair to get the laugh out. Once the shop calms down, Mitchell looks at Mike.

"In all seriousness tho, why get married now? I have to know." Mike takes a minute to think about the answer to Mitchell's question.

"Cause man, at the end of the day, Mia is a dope ass woman. I know that any dude would be lucky to have her, so if I gotta lock her down before some other nigga get her, then so be it."

Mitchell nods his head in understanding. In that moment, saying it out loud, Mike felt confident about his impulsive proposal. Mitchell interrupts Mike's thoughts, "So that means no more, uh what's the word. Sneaky links?" Mike abruptly cuts off Mitchell by putting his hand up.

"I said I'm gettin' married, I never said I was becoming a priest." Mitchell laughs, shaking his head at Mike as Mike explains himself.

"Look, like any of us here, I like a variety of 'poon and that's not gonna go away cause I put a ring on it. Mia knows the man she's marrying. She agreed to marry me while a naked chick was looking for her panties. She know what it is." One of the other barbers interjects with a question.

"You sure about that?" Confidently, Mike responds with a resounding, "Yes! She know what it is, so I'ma keep doin' me." A different man comments.

"Smart man, because sex stops the minute she says I Do!"

Mike looks terrified at the man's comment.

"Really?"

Hearing the sound of fear in Mike's voice, the other men laugh just as Terry, a former Atlanta Hawks basketball player sitting in the barber chair next to Mike, stands up when his barber takes the cape off.

"Com'on man, everybody know that. After the first 2 years, she's gonna want it less and less. Oh and don't have kids, you ain't never gonna get it."

Mike attempts to not let Terry's comment bother him, he brushes it off by responding, "Nah bruh, that might be your situation. Not mine."

"Aight," Terry responds, looking Mike dead in the eye.

Several other men chime in with their opinions.

"He right. I got married 22 years ago and had sex 22 times. And that was in the first 2 years, just like he said." Mitchell responds, "That because your wife came down with dementia in the third year and every time you tried she hollered rape." Everyone laughs again.

"Aye! Aye! All the charges were dropped. I'm good now." The men laugh even louder.

Terry pays his barber then waves to everyone as he makes his way to the exit.

"Aight folk, I'm gone."

Mike doesn't take his eyes off Terry as he leaves. If looks could kill, Mike would be standing trial very soon. For some reason, Mike felt the truth in Terry's words but was more upset at the audacity of Terry challenging his relationship like that. It doesn't help that Mike holds a tinge of jealousy toward Terry, with him being a former all-star ball player and all.

Mitchell turns Mike's chair around and leans in close to him, talking to him with intention.

"Listen young blood. I ain't sayin marriage isn't beautiful because it is. It's the best thing to have when you find someone worth it. But the sex does stop eventually and you have to love her enough to be OK with that. Take it from me. I been married 9 times." Mike's eyes widen.

"Damn OG, nine?!"

"Yep, every time the sex stopped with one, I got me a new one. Why you think I'm still cuttin' hair at my age? Alimony killin' me."

Mike belly laughs, throwing his head back just as Mitchell puts the clippers to his forehead.

"Stay still now before I mess this line up." Mike immediately straightens up.

"Oh nah, we can't do that."

Just like the barbershop, Mia's salon is just as posh. 2 years ago, Mike had given her the money to open it up in the heart of Atlanta's Castleberry Hill Arts District. She found an abandoned warehouse just before covid caused the city's real estate market to skyrocket. It took nearly seven months for Mia to rehab the space but it turned out exactly how she wanted it.

It's always been Mia's dream to be a business owner and she wanted her shop to be a one stop spot for all a woman's grooming needs. The front has 10 stations doing everything from styling, cutting, dying, weaves, locs and braids. In the middle of the shop is the nail section and in the back of the first floor, her employees do facials, lash extensions as well as eyebrow and yoni waxing. Upstairs Mia also created a small beauty school to teach young women and men not only how to do hair but how to run a business for themselves if that's what they eventually want to do.

While smooth early 2000's Neo soul music plays throughout the building, women are served mimosas while they wait for their appointment. Laughter fills the air in abundance, it's a vibe for sure.

It's the middle of the afternoon and Mia doesn't have a client for the next hour. She sits in her station's chair with a big smile on her face while she scrolls on her iPad looking at bridal dresses. She's elated, thoughts of walking down the aisle in the perfect dress haven't left her mind since Mike slid the ring on her finger.

Mia's best friend, Denise, stands at the section next to her braiding micro braids for her client. Denise's attention is divided between the woman's floor length braids and Mia's iPad. Mia lands on a dress and stares at it for a second. Denise says, "I like that one." Mia smiles big but quickly her face turns to confusion.

"Yeah, I keep going back to that one. It's between this one and this one." Mia shows Denise another dress.

Denise finishes the long braid and takes a minute to examine the other dress.

"Damn that's a tough one. I'd get'em both and do a wardrobe change. One for the ceremony and one for the reception." Mia replies, "I like that idea. But they're asking for a bag for them both."

"Oh girl please. Like Mike is gonna tell you no. He got it." Mia laughs.

"FACTS!" She and Denise high five and chuckle.

In the midst of their laughing, Natalie walks in strutting towards Mia as if she's on a runway. Natalie should have been a model and even though she's approaching 56, she can still make 20-year-olds re-evaluate their femininity, she's that stunning.

"MOMMY!!"

Mia sees Natalie coming, she leaps from her chair dropping her iPad. Luckily Denise catches it before it smashes on the floor. Mia throws her arms around her mother like a woman whose husband just came home from war. The two hug tightly and lovingly. Natalie asks, "How's my baby?" Mia breaks the hug and flashes the ring in her face.

"Engaged!" Mia does a cute little dance.

Natalie takes Mia by the hand, bringing the ring closer to her face. She looks at Mia, then at the ring, then looks at Denise with concern on her face. When Natalie looks at Denise, she drops her head and pretends to be wrapped up in braiding. Natalie curses her lips at Mia. That look deflates the wind from Mia's sails.

Natalie doesn't say a word. She drops Mia's hand then heads towards Mia's office. Confused, Mia looks at Denise. "What did I do?" Denise shakes her head while talking, "I don't know but hurry up and go get yelled at so you can tell me what she said."

"Really?"

Before Denise could answer, Natalie calls out Mia's name in a voice that every child knows isn't good when they hear it.

Natalie paces around Mia's office awaiting her to enter. Cautiously, Mia walks into her office with her shoulders slumped, head down and timid like a five-year-old. The second Mia enters, Natalie turns to her, "I won't allow it!"

Mia thought to herself, *won't allow what? Marry Mike? Ha!* Feeling herself, Mia straightens up and looks at Natalie and sees her as another grown woman and not her mother. This allows Mia to talk without fear of what would come once the words left her lips.

"With all due respect, I don't need your approval." Natalie folds her arms, she gasps clenching her imaginary pearls. She can't believe Mia just said that.

She attempts to say something but stops. She looks around the office gathering herself, slightly chuckling which makes Mia very nervous. Natalie takes a deep breath before she says, "Fine. Don't call me when he cheats on you again." "He already promised he wouldn't."

Natalie rolls her eyes then takes a seat on the edge of Mia's desk. Mia continues to plead her case.

"He's serious this time. And I believe him. He put a ring on it. He wouldn't have done that if he hadn't changed."

Natalie shakes her head looking at Mia with pity. "You sound just like Chrisean Rock. Stupid!"

Mia's mouth drops open. *How dare she*, she thought. Mia blurts out, "He's not daddy."

Just as quickly as the words escaped Mia's mouth she regretted it. She ducks in anticipation of the slap she was sure was coming her way. But it doesn't. Natalie looks at Mia.

"He's exactly like your father. That's how I know. I know what it looks like, can't you see that?"

Sincerity replaced the disappointment in Natalie's voice. She thought she'd be able to get through to Mia if she used honey instead of lava.

"It doesn't matter what you say. I'm marrying Mike. If you come to the wedding, cool. If not, well-."

Natalie stands, fixing the fit of her dress.

"What if he does it again?" Pretending to be 100% sure, Mia says, "He won't."

"But what if he does?" Natalie asks one last time before leaving the office.

Mia watches her mother walk through the salon and out the door. Her words echo in Mia's head over and over again. The walk back to her chair seemed like it was miles away. Mia could see some of her employees avoiding eye contact with her. She was sure they all heard the conversation through the door. It's not like the salon is soundproof.

When she finally makes it back to her station, Mia flops down, pouting. Denise looks over at Mia. Mia feels Denise's eyes on her. Without looking at Denise, Mia says, "Go ahead and say it."

One of Mia's employees brings her a mimosa served on a purple and gold trimmed serving tray. As Mia drinks the mimosa in one gulp, Denise says, "I usually don't get in between you and your mother, but a real friend would say, she's right. Have you asked yourself what *if* he cheats again? Before he's married? Hell after he's married. What would you do?" Already irritated with her mother, Mia snaps at Denise.

"What would you do? Oh that's right, you're the side chick."

Mia leaps from her chair and storms out of the salon. Denise talks at Mia despite her already having left.

"Oh I see you chose violence today huh!?"

Chapter 2

In a quiet and quaint suburban neighborhood in the Kirkwood section of Atlanta, a moving truck drives down the residential street. Behind it, Mike and Mia's Mercedes S580 follows.

The truck pulls into the driveway of a large single family multi-floor home. The house is the envy of every house in the neighborhood as it's not designed like a typical home. Its rooftop patio is just the beginning of its originality. The home is mostly made of 2-way glass with a 20-foot keyless door. It sits on a bed of manicured Kentucky Bluegrass with the Platinum Trust Realty sold sign, the only thing disrupting its beauty.

Before the car could come to a complete stop, Mia jumps out. To say she's excited is an understatement. She doesn't take her eyes off the house, her ear-to-ear smile only gets bigger with each passing second. *Could this really be real? Am I really a married woman? Is this my house?* Mia thought to herself. Mike exits the car and stands beside Mia. She looks at him with schoolgirl admiration, she interlocks her fingers with his. They both look at their wedding rings. Mia jokes, "I guess this house isn't the only thing off the market." Mike awkwardly chuckles.

If Mia's excitement is at a ten then Mike's is at a two. Looking at the rings and the house he dropped a small fortune on, it's starting to settle in for Mike. This is now his life. Mike and Mia had separate apartments while dating, Mike would bring his sneaky links to his place when Mia was at work. His only mistake, giving her a key.

But now that they shared a home, the only thing running through Mike's mind was where would he bring the women now? Then he remembered, he still has his condo! A sinister delighted smile slivers across Mike's face. He leans over, hugging Mia.

"This is our forever home baby!" Mia exclaimed. Mike looks Mia in her eyes and says, "Forever isn't long enough."

Mia squeals with joy planting a big kiss on Mike. He always knew what to say to get that type of reaction out of Mia. She falls for it every time, boosting Mike's devious confidence.

Mike opens his eyes during their kiss. Scanning his surroundings his eyes land on a vision. Jogging down the street toward them was a beautiful big breasted woman with smooth caramel skin. The woman wears an almost too small sports bra exposing her toned stomach and her leggings shape her Nikki Minaj sized butt perfectly as her hair blows in the wind. She makes eye contact with Mike and instinctively smiles seductively at him. In his head,

Mike sees flashes of him kissing the arch of her back as he makes his way lower, smiling as she moans with pleasure. He pictures what she would look like naked.

A flawless coke bottled body without a stitch of hair kneeling down in between his legs. He feels the warmth of her mouth. Saliva dripping down his pole and her hair tickles his inner thighs as she bobs up and down wildly.

Mike abruptly breaks the kiss with Mia. She feels his heart racing, he's breathing heavily. Mia looks at him concerned. She asks, "What's wrong?" Mike watches the woman jog across the street then turns his attention back to Mia. He stutters his response, "Uhh, nothing. Com'on, let's go in."

Mia smiles, jumping in place excited. Mike grabs her by the hand leading her toward the house.

A few weeks later, Mike and Mia are fully settled in their lavish home. They spared no expense with the decor. It's a mix of sophisticated modern luxury with a hint of extravagance.

Their housewarming party is a classy vibe situation. People congregate in various rooms talking to each other, laughing, eating and drinking while music plays through the speakers inconspicuously built into the walls. Together, Mike and Mia work the room, hugging, smiling and shaking hands from people who all congratulate them on their new home. New people enter the home placing gifts on the table in the foyer.

From the open concept kitchen, Denise calls for Mia. She kisses Mike before leaving him with a group of his male friends and heads toward Denise.

"I think it's done." Denise says as she sits at the granite oversized island pouring herself a glass of wine.

Mia puts on a pair of oven mitts then takes a hot pan of finger foods out of the oven. Struggling to hold it, she searches around the cluttered counters for a place to put the pan but they're all filled with a variety of delectable edibles.

Denise is too engulfed texting on her phone to see Mia needs help. Mia sees a place to put the pan but needs to create space. She looks at Denise.

"Hey, can you move that over for me so I can sit this down?" Denise holds up her glass and her phone.

"My hands are full too." Mia shakes her head, chuckles then uses her elbow to make room for the pan. She sets it down, then leans on the counter talking as she tries to catch her breath.

"Girl I can't with you." Denise looks up from her phone with a matter of fact look on her face.

"Next time you do your Ciara prayer, ask for a maid." They share a laugh. Mia begins to plate some of the food.

"Trust me, I have everything I need."

Mia looks up looking at Mike in another room. The two make eye contact. Mike smiles and waves. Mia gushes. Denise sees, pretends to gag. Mia is not amused. Denise is a great friend to Mia but there is no love lost toward Mike.

"Oh would you cut it out?" Mia asks. Denise puts her phone down, she leans over the island whispering.

"I love you but I can't help it. I still feel some type of way about how he paused during his vows."

"Girl! He did not pause!" Mia exclaims.

In the other room, Mike talks to his childhood friend Clive, a fashionably dressed 30 something with looks that could rival Mike's. The two converse, chuckling at Clive's recap of Mike's vow debacle.

"That was the longest pause I've seen at a wedding, ever! It was like time stopped. The matrix glitched. I think I might have dozed off." The men share a laugh, Mike playfully hits Clive in the arm.

"Yeah man, I don't even know what happened. It's like I heard the words and my brain turned off."

Clive looks at his wife Michelle talking to another woman across the room. He smiles and nods at her. She blows him a kiss. Then turns back to Mike.

"Me and Michelle was looking at Mia's mom just waiting for her to run up to that altar and give you all the smoke." Mike rubs his head exhaling deeply.

"Yo her mom is no joke!"

Back in the kitchen, Mia and Denise's conversation takes an unexpected turn. This time, Denise is not amused by what Mia is saying, "Oh you got jokes. What I look like dating one of Mike's friends?" Denise shakes her head no.

"I do NOT date dudes with a lot of male friends." Mia looks perplexed.

"Why not? Better than them having a bunch of thirst traps in they face." Denise replies with, "Cause dudes with a lot of male friends have too many alibis."

Mia bursts into laughter causing people to turn their attention to her hoping to get in on what's funny. Mia waves the onlookers off, she politely tells them it's nothing. Denise continues talking, doubling down on her statement. "I'm serious. If he got a lot of male friends he a hoe. If he got a lot of female friends he's a super hoe. But if he keeps to himself and don't have a lot of niggas in his ear he's- ," Mia interrupts, "Jeffery Dameur?"

Mike and Clive continue talking to each other. Mike's taken aback when Clive questioned if he could be faithful in his marriage.

"Bruh, I can be faithful!" Mike proclaims. Clive laughs and continues to give Mike a hard time.

"Aahhh, you said you CAN, not you Will. It's all good bruh, you ain't gotta convince me. I know what it is. It's just not in you."

Never one to back down from a challenge, Mike fights to convince Clive that being faithful would be easy. Clive, having known Mike for most of his life, just couldn't pass up the opportunity to challenge him on that.

"Aight then, put some money up!"

Mike reaches into his pocket, more than happy to put his money where his mouth is. That is until he looked at the overconfident smile on Clive's face, that got him to thinking. Ultimately, Mike knows himself and part of that is knowing he loves pussy just a little bit more than money. Especially if he's gonna bet against it, the odds are against the house on this one. Besides, with all the new women in his house for the party, Mike's cheated seven times in his head already. Who was he fooling?

A woman Mike has never met before walks past him and Clive, both men check her out. Then Clive catches himself looking and he turns away. He peaks out the side of his eye to see Mike staring hard. In an attempt to get him to stop, Clive hits Mike in the arm.

"Damn bruh, what you do that for?"

"You was lookin' a little too hard my boy." Nervously Mike looks toward the kitchen and sees Mia laughing with Denise. He breathes a sigh of relief knowing Mia didn't see him. Clive shakes his head at Mike and the two share a laugh.

"You gonna get in trouble in ya own crib." Mike replies, "Oh no. That's sneaky link rule number one. You don't creep where you eat." Clive chuckles rolling his eyes at the rule.

"Not rules." Mike nods his head yes.

"Yep and there's nine more. They're just like the Biggie song. But instead of crack commandments it's commandments guaranteed not to get you caught up."

Clive can't believe his ears. Mike has said some wild stuff in the past but this is new. Most of the time Clive just took what Mike was saying as him just talking shit but strangely enough Clive realized that Mike is dead serious. Clive doesn't share Mike's cavalier attitude about cheating but he couldn't really say much against it. You know, bro code and all. A thought crept into Clive's mind and he just spit it out. "You ever thought about being polyamorous?" Mike lets out a loud laugh.

Quickly he covers his mouth while still laughing. Mia walks over to Mike and Clive carrying a hookah. Mikes' eyes light up.

"Thanks babe, you must've read my mind." Mia lovingly smiles.

"Yeah, yeah but I better not see no burn marks on my carpet."

Clive nudges Mike. Mike looks at him shaking his head no. Mia looks at them both suspiciously.

"What's going on here?" She asks.

Mike stammers as he struggles to decide to say what Clive wants him to say. Mia smiles, "Oh just say it."

Mike looks around the room in fear of someone catching wind of something that would later be used as gossip. Despite his philandering way, Mike never wants to embarrass Mia.

Seeing the coast is clear, he says, "Babe, how do you feel about polyamory?" Without skipping a beat, Mia replies, "I don't know. How many years does a double homicide get you?" Clive laughs, "Damn Mia, you ain't gotta kill them." Mia looks Clive up and down, playfully but in a serious manner.

"Oh no, not the woman. I mean you and Mike." Clive laughs, confused.

"Why me?"

"Where else would Mike get a dumbass idea like that if not from you. Michelle! Come get ya man." Mia yells across the room as she points at Clive before walking away. Mike hits Clive in the chest.

"Aye, don't be gettin' me in trouble." Clive replies, "Nah, you're gonna do that all by yourself."

To Mike, the idea of polyamory never entered his mind. There was one time early in their relationship when Mike suggested the two go to a swinger's club but that didn't end well. He had a split bottom lip for a week.

Mike and Mia have been settled in their new home for a few weeks now and by all accounts, Mike has been faithful. But not by choice. He hasn't been able to get the image of that sexy neighbor he saw jogging on the day they moved in. He hasn't seen her since and it's not due to his lack of trying. He checks the mailbox several times a day as an excuse to get out of the house. He drives slowly in and out of the neighborhood and has started jogging twice a day hoping to catch a glimpse of her.

Unbeknownst to Mike however, today his efforts would pay off. Mike decided to take the morning off and left out of his house for his morning jog. It was later than he normally leaves out as he slept in a little later. Mia pushed back her first client of the day so the two could have breakfast together without having to rush out.

While Mike jogs down the street, music blasting through his headphones, Mia drives up beside him on her way to the salon. She rolled down her window and honked the horn to get his attention. When Mike looks over, Mia smiles, blows him a kiss then waves him goodbye before driving off.

He smiles then continues his run thinking to himself. Would it really be so bad being with one woman for the rest of his life? I mean, Mia is a great woman, isn't that what every man wants? *Do better Mike*, he thinks to himself. Then in that moment, Mike decided to listen to his inner self. From this moment on, he was going to be faithful.

Mike jogs around the corner too deep in his thoughts to see he is about to run into someone. Mike collides into a woman. They both fall to the ground, Mike hitting his head on the pole of the stop sign. Disoriented he looks up and he can't believe his eyes. Through his temporary double vision Mike looks at the face in front of him.

His heart jumps, it's the woman he's been searching for for weeks. What are the odds? Just when he decided to be faithful, Mike literally fell into some pussy. Go figure. She raises her eyebrow, Mike now with regular vision smiles licking his lips and next thing you know, Mike is staring up at her beautiful surgical D cup titis bouncing up and down.

She's as perfect as Mike imagined she would be. He palms her supple ass with both hands controlling her movement, he thrusts and goes deeper.

"Oh my god! Oh my god!" She moans.

Mike thrusts harder and faster causing her to get louder. Her body begins to tremble. Mike knows this means she's moments away from climaxing. He consciously maintains his thrusting and smacks her ass hard. The sound echoes throughout the room. She takes one of Mike's hands and places it around her neck. He obliges. She commands, "Call me a whore!"

Whoa! Mike is shocked at that. Unsure if he should actually call her a whore he says nothing. She commands him again.

"CALL ME A WHORE!"

She smacks Mike across the face. He's livid.

"BITCH!" he yells out. Expecting her to get upset, she surprises him with her response.

"Yeah! I'm a dirty little bitch!"

The side of his face stings, Mike feels just how hard she hit him, however, he realizes she likes it rough so he joins in.

Mike calls her every name under the sun, each time he does the wilder she gets. Mike feels her getting wetter, the sound of his nine inches smacking against her insides makes the desired macaroni and cheese sound that every man likes. He looks down smiling when he sees her juices pouring out of her and down the shaft of his dick.

She screams out then unexpectedly she leaps off his dick standing over him screaming in ecstasy as she vigorously rubs her pussy squirting all over Mikes' face and chest. When she's done, she falls on top of Mike trying to catch her breath.

Mike lays there soaking wet, her hair covering half his face, trying to wrap his mind around what just happened. Then she begins to snore.

"What the hell?" Mike says.

He moves her hair out of his face looking down at her in disbelief.

"Oh hell nah."

Mike taps her back continuously trying to wake her back up. After a few moments he stops, feeling defeated. He exhales loudly out of frustration. He didn't finish.

Mike's going through a wave of different emotions. On one hand he's still not over the fact he just had the best sexual experience he's had in weeks but it's overshadowed by the overwhelming feeling of guilt. During his jog he thought he was making progress when he decided not to cheat and not only a minute later he was thigh deep in another woman.

This was his first time cheating while being married to Mia. For whatever reason, this feels different. For the first time he genuinely feels like he did something wrong. Worst even, he doesn't know how to come back from it. His continued thoughts make him nervous. If he feels this strongly on the inside, would Mia be able to pick up on it?

Mike stops at a red light on Lenox road. He rolls down his car window taking in a deep breath as the sounds of the city pour into the car. He looks around trying to figure out what his next move is going to be. His eyes land on the Lenox mall parking lot. Nothing gets a woman's mind off the idea of you cheating on her like an unexpected expensive gift. He knows what he's going to do.

As soon as the light turns green Mike speeds ahead of the person in the right lane speeding into the mall parking lot. He sticks his middle finger out the window toward the car aggressively honking their horn.

Mike stands perplexed in front of a wall of purses inside the Louis Vuitton store. He's never bought Mia a purse before. Matter of fact, he's never bought Mia anything. Typically he'd just give her his black card and tell her not to break the bank. When he bought the engagement ring it was completely by accident when he was buying himself a new watch. He gets the sense that he is in foreign territory and remembers why he hates shopping. He doesn't even buy his own clothes.

Luckily for him a well-dressed salesclerk approaches him just as he's about to grab a random purse and get outta there. Out of his peripheral Mike sees the clerk coming his way. He looks him up and down and immediately makes it up in his mind the clerk is gay. Why? It's Atlanta, he's dressed way too well to be a man's man and he works in a store catered to women.

The clerk asks in a non-threatening voice, "Is there something I can help you with, sir?"

Mike doesn't look at the clerk but responds in a passive aggressive manner.

"No offense but I think I should ask a woman's opinion." Mike looks around, spots a female sales clerk almost finished ringing up a customer.

"I'll wait until she's done."

Mike assumed he said enough to sway the salesclerk to leave but it doesn't work. Like any good salesman, he's persistent.

"Until then, allow me to try. Are you looking for a gift for a specific occasion? Anniversary? Birthday? Or just because?"

Determined to be more direct in his unwillingness to allow the male sales clerk to help, he turns to him but he changes course. He looks down at the sales clerk's shoes. Despite his metro sexual attire, he's rocking a limited pair of Christian Dior Jordan 1's. Mike raises an eyebrow impressed. He immediately changes his mind, making a joke in the process.

"Maybe you can help me. You look like you've cheated on a few women in your day." The clerk chuckles.

"Bad women are like pollen, they're everywhere." Mike lets out a genuine laugh, his defenses and reservations about the clerk have disappeared.

"Facts. So what gift says I'm sorry I fucked our neighbor three months after our wedding and moving into our forever home?"

The salesclerk blinks a few times, swallows hard then adjusts his suit. He chuckles a little, causing Mike to join in. Mike shows the clerk his black card. Instantly the clerk nods.

"That has been known to fix countless problems. Follow me. Our private selection is right this way."

Mike sits with his legs crossed, drink in his hand and a satisfied expression on his face. *Who knew shopping was this cool. Now I see why women like it so much,* he thought to himself. Engulfed in his own thoughts and the king treatment he's receiving, Mike couldn't make out what the salesclerk was saying about an expensive purse he was holding up in front of Mike's face.

Mike doesn't know anything about purses, he just knows brand names. How he sees it, the more expensive the item, the better it must be and the more Mia will like it. Mike interrupts the salesclerk by blurting out, "I'll take it!"

Mike nervously paces around the kitchen island. The LV bag sits on top of the island next to the iPad open on a screen about polygamy. Mike and the salesclerk had an interesting conversation while he was being run up. He expressed to Mike how he and his wife became polygamous a few years ago and it saved their marriage.

Any other day Mike would have brushed it off knowing Mia wouldn't go for it. But it hit harder because Mike remembered Clive also spoke about it at their housewarming party, and it got him thinking. When he mentioned it to Mia it was said almost in a joking manner, kinda testing the waters. She knew he wasn't serious so she responded the way she did. But what if now Mike is serious?

Mike tries to rationalize the situation laying out just the facts and the facts are, for the foreseeable future he's not going to stop fuckin' other women. That's just it, no matter what. Another fact is, he does want to be faithful to Mia, unfortunately, the math ain't mathin'. The only way Mike can do both is if he and Mia engage in a poly lifestyle.

After several drinks and a deep dive on the internet about polyamory, Mike had his mind made up. He was going to give the purse to Mia, buttering her up, then he would lay it on her. In his mind, if she went with it, cool, problem solved. But if she doesn't then he'll continue doing what he's doing and he'll be a frequent shopper at the LV store.

For what seemed like an eternity to Mike, Mia finally walks through the front door. She calls for his name from the foyer, he responds, "I'm in the kitchen."

Mike takes a deep breath and ensures the LV bag is positioned just right so it's the first thing she sees when she walks in. Mike can hear Mia's heels hitting their hardwood floor, she's getting closer. She's saying something but Mike can't hear her over his loud erratic heartbeat. She enters the kitchen tossing her purse on the island but her eyes are fixated on the fridge.

She snatches the door open, pulls out the bottom drawer and picks up the first bottle of wine she sees. She continued to talk, and suddenly, Mike could hear every word.

"I tried calling you this afternoon, where were you?" She asks as she takes a wine class from the cabinet she could barely reach. Mike watches her pour the wine, she hasn't looked in his direction or the direction of the LV bag since she's walked in. He replies, "I was at the mall."

Mia finally looks up, she makes eye contact with a raised eyebrow.

"Really? You hate shopping."

Then her eyes land on the LV bag. She takes a big gulp of the wine, smiles as she wipes a drop from her lips.

"That's for me?" Mike nervously nods yes.

Mia puts the wine glass and bottle down and belines for the bag. Carefully she removes the heavy box from the bag. She sets it down on the island gently rubbing her hand over the words on top of it. She looks at Mike, like a child on Christmas, then she slowly removes the box top.

She moves the tissue paper revealing the purse, her eyes light up.

"OMG! Babe, this is beautiful! You've never bought me a purse before? What's the occasion?" Mia picks up the purse, examining it, hugging it.

Mike doesn't respond, he just looks down at the tablet. Mia follows his eyes. Her eyes land on the headline of the article on the tablet. Her expression goes from 100 to zero real quick as she stares at it. She lets the purse drop back into the box. She looks at Mike, furious.

"Gimmie ya phone," she demands. Mike's confused. "Huh?" Mia barks back.

"You heard what the fuck I said." Mia charges Mike trying to get to his pockets but Mike fights her off proclaiming there's nothing in his phone. Mia doesn't care, nor does she believe him. After a few seconds of struggling, Mike gives in, throwing his hands up allowing Mia to retrieve his phone from his back pocket.

She walks to the other side of the island putting distance between them as she scrolls through Mike's messages and call log. She finds nothing. Frustrated, she slams the phone on the island and looks at Mike, visibly upset and sad.

"I just don't get it. I thought we were happy," she says as she flops down into the bar stool. Mike consciously chooses his next words wisely.

"We are but sometimes I want more. This isn't cheating."

Mia looks at Mike as if he has three heads. *What the hell does he mean this isn't cheating*, she thought to herself.

"Why? Because I'll know about it?" she asks. Mike nods his head yes. Mia sighs, putting her head in her hands. "When I think about spending the rest of my life with you, that thought doesn't include another bitch. Whether I know about them or not."

Mike rubs his head, not sure what to say. Mia gets up slowly making her way over to Mike. Mike tenses up bracing himself to get hit but Mia stops in front of him. She sincerely looks deep into his eyes and speaks with a calm soft voice, her voice cracks a little.

"Are you not attracted to me anymore?" Mike takes Mia's hands holding them to his chest. His tone matches hers.

"Of course I am."

"So am I not enough for you, sexually? Or are you completely incapable of keeping your dick out of other bitches?"

Mike doesn't know how to respond, he drops his head. Mia snatches her hands away taking a few steps back. She looks back at the LV box, she scoffs.

"That's what this is all about? This is your way of apologizing for doing it again, isn't it?"

Knowing his only option is to keep it 100 with her but unable to find the words that wouldn't piss her off, Mike merely shrugs.

"What do you want from me Mia?" Instantly she says, "Monogamy."

Mia snatches the box and bag from the island and storms out of the kitchen. Mike watches Mia leave. He wants to say something but can't seem to find the right words. He thinks he's overplayed his hand but quickly brushes it off knowing deep down that Mia isn't going to leave. Hell, she caught him with his dick in his hand literally and she agreed to marry him. She'll just be mad for the night and be regular old Mia in the morning. No harm. No foul.

Mike's phone chimes, he gets a text message. He looks toward the stairs ensuring Mia is gone before he looks at it. A smile slithers across his face as he looks at the naked picture from the neighbor. Another text comes through stating the front door is open and she's waiting for him. Mike finishes his drink , shakes off the interaction with Mia then sends a reply.

Mia slams the door shut in their bedroom then flops on the bed letting the LV bag drop from her hand onto the floor. She buries her face in her hands, muffling her sobbing. She can't believe Mike wants to have sex with other women. Surely, she thought after they were married Mike's sexual appetite would be satisfied with just what she was serving him. The harsh reality that isn't the case eats at Mia and she doesn't know how to react.

She takes her phone from her purse about to send a text message to Denise when she hears the front door close. Confused, she stops the text, listens. She doesn't hear any sounds coming from downstairs. No voices. Could someone have come to the house? No, no one rang the doorbell.

While questions whirl in Mia's mind, she hears a car turn over. The headlights shine through the windows in the bedroom causing Mia to shield her eyes. *Oh hell naw*, she thought to herself. She leaps from the bed walking over to the window peering out just in time to see Mike's car back out of the driveway.

She thinks to herself, where the hell is he going at this time of night? Sadness creeps over her as she realizes ain't nothing open this time of night except Waffle House and legs. Could Mike be this disrespectful to leave out to go get a piece of ass while his wife is crying alone in their marital bed? Of course he can be.

As she watches Mike's tail lights disappear in the night, Mia's chest tightens, her body grows hot and she fans herself while sliding down the wall to the floor. Thoughts of leaving engage in a tug of war with the thought of going Angela Bassett waiting to exhale on his clothes and shoes. But what would that solve if she isn't going to leave?

Defeated, Mia kicks and screams loudly. Her scream echoes throughout the large room and hallway. She stops when her eyes land on the LV bag sitting on the floor seemingly teasing her as it sits a few feet away from her.

She aggressively wipes the tears from her face then crawls over to the bag, staring at it. Thinking if she should open it or throw it away. After what seemed like an eternity, she decides she can't bring herself to do either. Mia composes herself, stands and slowly picks up the LV bag.

Like a poised woman, she walks out of the bedroom with her head held high.

She enters one of the guest bedrooms that's decorated like a restoration hardware showroom floor, the LV bag swaying with each step. She stops in front of the closet door. Mia knows Mike doesn't come into any of the other rooms and he's so self-centered, he wouldn't even realize she's not using the purse. It'll be fine in here.

She looks down at the bag, one more thought of opening it enters her mind but she ignores it, she opens the closet door instead. She turns on the light revealing the closet being completely empty. She walks inside and gently places the bag in the back of the closet in a corner. Satisfied, she steps out of the closet, looking at it one last time before turning off the light and shutting the door.

Back in her bedroom Mia sits at her vanity tying her hair up. She's made a decision, she will not excuse Mike's infidelity with lavish empty I'm sorry gifts. She also understands that's not going to do anything to stop him. He doesn't mind spending the money if he thinks it's doing something. But she will not play the role of the happy complacent wife anymore either.

Mia swallows a tough pill behind the understanding that Mike didn't really want to be married, he just wanted to lock Mia down. He's for the streets, she's not. So if that's what this sham of a marriage really is, then fine, she'll be on lockdown. But also her pussy is on lockdown. The cooking is on lockdown. The cleaning is on lockdown. Her silence is on lockdown. Every time Mike comes out his mouth sideways, especially in public, she isn't going to let it wait until they get home to address it like a "good wife" should. No! He's going to get the smoke immediately.

And why not? He already has her looking crazy in these streets so why not lean into it. In her mind, there are only two outcomes to her planned pettiness. Either Mike is going to get tired of the embarrassment and her wifely withdrawal or he's going to realize what he has and finally learn to appreciate her or divorce her. Which will only work out in Mia's favor, financially. Oh wait, there's a third option which consists of slow singing, flower bringing and their tragic outcome being reenacted on an episode of Snapped.

With that, Mia is at peace and accepts whichever option reveals itself, whenever that may be. As she finishes tying her hair up, she looks at herself in the mirror. She smiles at her reflection, knowing and feeling beautiful. Sexy. Her eyes examine her neck lined down to the middle of her slightly exposed breasts.

She slowly removes her silk kimono off each of her shoulders, it slides down resting on her waist. She runs the tip of her index fingernail down the top of her breasts and down to her nipples. She slowly circles her nipples realizing she hasn't pleasured herself since college and it's been a few weeks since Mike sweated her hair out and left her in the wet spot spread out like a starfish.

At the memory of having repeated orgasms, Mia pinches her nipples, letting out a sensual sound of pleasure. Her hands inch their way down her stomach, past her belly button then between her legs. She enters herself, closing her eyes and throws her head back envisioning Mike's hands gently stroking her lips.

The familiar feeling of clitoris stimulation takes over Mia's entire body. She feels the sticky goddess nectar run down her hand turning her on more. She can feel Mike's warm breath and tongue spelling her name between her legs until something unusual happens. Mike's face disappears from Mia's mind.

Mia opens her eyes looking down between her spread legs and sees the top of the head of an unknown man. The unknown man looks up at Mia, the two make eye contact. Mia's so startled and frightened that she backs away from the illusion and falls onto the floor landing hard on her back.

Mia's mind searches for any explanation for what just happened. She's never thought about another man let alone fantasized about one. What does this mean? Does this mean she wants another man? Oh God, did she just emotionally cheat on her husband? Mia shakes off the random thoughts as she gets off the floor, wiping her wet fingers on her kimono.

Chapter 3

Mike sits in Dr. Phil's office rocking himself back and forth as he attempts to piece together his next sentence. He looks at Dr. Phil and says, "I'm not a fuck boy OK? It's just something about knowing when you get home, a loving woman is gonna be there. All these other women are temporary. But it doesn't mean I love Mia any less."

Mike takes a beat from his rant, searching Dr. Phil's face for reassurance, but he doesn't give it to him.

"You say you're not a fuck boy but your actions speak otherwise."

Mike is surprised at Dr. Phil's bluntness. His eyes widen as he proclaims, "But I'm really not!"

Dr. Phil rubs his forehead letting out an exhausted sigh. Then he looks Mike dead in the eyes and asks, "Then why are you cheating on, as you put it, a loving wife?" Mike stands, pacing around the office searching the air for a logical explanation for his actions.

"I honestly don't see it as cheating. I'm not cheating, technically." Dr. Phil looks at Mike as confused as anyone would after hearing of Mike's continued exploits.

Dr. Phil asks Mike to elaborate on his statement. Mike sits back down, he says, "OK, let me ask you. In your professional opinion, what's the main things a woman wants from a man?"

Dr. Phil answers without hesitation as he's confident in his response.

"Security, protection, knowing she'd be taken care of financially."

Mike leaps from the chair again, rejuvenated.

"Exactly! And what's the main thing a man wants from a woman?" Mike asks. Again, without hesitation, Dr. Phil answers with, "Love, a homemaker, someone who nurtures him." Mike yells loud and obnoxiously, "WRONG!"

Dr. Phil jumps backward in his seat, taken aback by Mike's sudden outburst. Seeing that he frightened the good doctor, Mike calms down, returning to his normal tone.

"I'm not saying those things aren't great to have. But the main thing, the number one thing a man wants from his woman is for her to be attractive and to be sexually available."

Now Dr. Phil is really confused. He takes a minute to think. Mike is smiling thinking he's just given Dr. Phil something he's never thought about. It's not that Dr. Phil is trying to process some new groundbreaking information, he's thinking of a way to challenge Mike without making him feel like the idiot he sounds like. Finally he says, "But Mia is sexually available."

Frustrated that Dr. Phil isn't picking up what he's putting down, Mike flops back into the chair and tries to explain it in more detail.

"All the main things Mia wants from me, I give to her and no one else. If I were providing those things to other women, then yes, I'd be cheating. But to most women sex may be in the middle if not at the end of the list. So if I have sex with other women, it's technically not considered cheating."

Dr. Phil raises an eyebrow. He's understood what Mike has been trying to say all along, however, Dr. Phil thinks it's the dumbest thing he's heard all year but he can't tell Mike that. Instead, he jots down in his notebook.

Mike leans back in his chair taking Dr. Phil's silence as confirmation that his ideology is correct. Dr. Phil's watch beeps, he looks at Mike, "That's our time. See you next week?" Mike sits in the chair thinking. Then he looks at Dr. Phil, "Aye doc. Am I making progress here?" Before Dr. Phil could answer, Mike says, "Know what? Never mind, we'll talk about it next week. I gotta get to my barber appointment and you know how this Atlanta traffic is. Catch you later."

Mike leaves the office with a pep in his step. Dr. Phil watches him leave then says to himself, "My new book is going to be a best seller thanks to that fool there."

Back in his sanctuary, the barbershop, Mike is getting his second line up in a week. Every man within earshot is hanging on Mike's every word as if he's a charismatic Baptist preacher. Even his elder wiser barber agrees. "Yeah that sounds about right." Mike responds, "Exactly."

A listener chimes in with his own statement.

"Yeah but try telling a woman that though. Then you're every name in the book." Mike wholeheartedly agrees. "Right! See, women can take away sex anytime they want for any reason. Oh I got a headache, oh I'm tired, oh it's my period. Blah, blah, blah. But as men we can't not pay the mortgage if we don't *"feel like it"*. If someone breaks into the house, we can't refuse to protect her cause I'm tired from work all day. We can't take days off from giving her the main things she needs. But the main thing we want is that we can be denied at any point and we can't say shit."

All the men in the barbershop nod and agree with each other. Another listener stands up like he caught the holy ghost.

"Bruh, you need a TedTalk."

The barbershop erupts in laughter just as Terry walks into the barbershop. Instantly Mike's mood changes but he makes sure it doesn't show on his face as Terry approaches him. The two men dap, Mike asks him how's it going. Terry responds, "I can't call it. How's married life?"

The men chuckle. Terry looks at everyone obviously left out of the joke. He asks, "What I miss?"

A man tells Mike to explain to Terry what he just told everyone. Mike smiles, looks over at Terry, "Aight, it's like this."

Terry listens as the barber lines him up. Mike, now finished with his line up, stands in the middle of the barbershop with every eye on him and every ear attentively listening. Word for word, Mike tells Terry what he told Dr. Phil and the other men who listen like it's the first time they're hearing it.

When he's done, the men applaud but Terry doesn't. Mike looks at Terry, Terry thinks, nods his head, he agrees. Mike claps his hands together happily smiling at the fact Terry agrees. *Terry might not be so bad after all*, Mike thinks to himself. Terry finally breaks his silence, "You said some real shit bruh, I can't hold you." Mike continues, "Cause it's facts. Any real man gonna agree."

Mike checks his watch, "Aight fellas I gotta get outta here. Ya'll be safe."

The men say their goodbyes as Mike leaves the barbershop. Once he's gone, the men continue with the conversation.

The house is quiet, only the occasional sounds of a fork and knife scraping across a plate interrupts the silence. Mia sits on the head of the dining room table alone eating dinner, it's halfway gone. She savors the last sip of her red wine then leans back in the chair satisfied. She hears the keypad on the front door beep six times. She smiles to herself knowing what's about to happen.

Mike bops into the house, still with a pep in his step like a man who's walking back to the village after slaying a lion. He finds Mia in the dining room.

"Hey babe," he says as he leans in for a kiss on Mia's lips. She turns her head away, giving Mike her cheek. She turns her face up but Mike doesn't notice as he walks into the kitchen, she shakes her head, wiping her face disgusted.

Mike enters the kitchen heading toward the overhead microwave. He opens it then his pep and smile quickly fade when he sees there's nothing there. He smacks his teeth then re-enters the dining room with his hands up confused.

"Aye! You didn't make me a plate?"

Mia puts the napkin down, looks up at Mike, unbothered. She responds in a condescending tone.

"I figured you had all you can eat already."

Mike is even more confused now.

"What does that mean?" Mia folds her hands resting her chin on them. She looks at Mike with a forced smile, she's about to say just what she means but she won't allow Mike to see she's hurt by it.

"It means I can smell what you ate, it's all in your beard."

Mike looks busted, checks his beard. *Damn*, Mike thinks. G*ot caught slippin' again. Got's to be more careful.* Mia stands from the table with a half-eaten plate of food in her hand. She walks right past Mike without saying a word, into the kitchen. Mike desperately tries to recover.

"Babe."

Mia holds up her hand shaking her head no. Mike stops talking. She opens the lid to the trash and scrapes the food into it. Mike can't believe what she's doing.

"WHOOOOAAA! I woulda ate that!"

Mia hands the empty plate to Mike along with the fork, then looks him in the eye.

"And that's why I threw it away." Mia brushes past him leaving the kitchen.

Mike doesn't follow her. He looks down at the empty plate then at Mia as she heads upstairs. Finally he responds, "Oh so that's what we doin'?" Mia responds without turning around.

"Yep!"

Mike nods his head then speaks in a Scarface voice, "OK! You wanna play rough? I CAN PLAY ROUGH!" He listens as Mia's footsteps get quieter as they reach the top. Then his stomach rumbles.

Mike puts the plate in the sink then opens the fridge looking for yesterday's leftovers or anything he can eat that doesn't require the use of the stove. He finds nothing. He slams the door shut, frustrated. His stomach rumbles again. Mike takes out his phone and opens the Uber eats app. Unbeknownst to Mike, Mia's cold shoulder has just started to freeze over.

In the bedroom Mia snickers uncontrollably, the look on Mike's face when she threw the food away is priceless. She starts to undress with a permanent smile on her face, proud of herself that she actually went through with it and didn't fold. If she's being honest with herself, a little piece of her feels guilty for leaving her husband hungry. Her mother always told her not to let a man leave the house horny or hungry. The way she sees it, if he's leaving to another woman with his balls empty then making sure his stomach is full is also her responsibility. Period!

Why should she be expected to honor her vows and so-called wifely duties if he isn't performing like a husband? For the first time in months, Mia feels vindicated, even if it came from something so small as not cooking for Mike. Mia is determined to make Mike realize that what he thinks he's getting outside of her is nothing in comparison to what he'll miss from her. Let the games begin!

Later that night, Mike takes a shower as his cell phone sits on the edge of the sink. Mia enters the bathroom, with a seductive look on her face. She removes her shirt and is about to unbutton her pants when Mike's phone chimes. Mike doesn't hear. Mia looks down at the phone, sees a text from a woman's name. She opens the text and sees nude pictures of the woman. Mia opens the shower looking at Mike with her seductive face, the face Mike knows means he's about to get some ass. Mia leans in front of him, her breasts pressed against Mike's chest, he smiles. Then Mia turns the shower knob hard to the right then quickly runs out of the shower pressing her back against the door.

Cold water pours from the rainwater shower head and Mike screams as the water beats over his body. He tries and fails at pushing Mia from the shower door. She's laughing loudly as Mike beats on the glass shower door as if he's trying to break it. In between her laughter, Mia yells over Mike's screams, "Just turn it back to hot genius."

Mike hears her and quickly turns the knob back to the hot water side. He exhales, spinning around trying to get warm again. Mia sinisterly stands outside the shower looking at him shivering. Finally warm again, Mike looks over at Mia as she stares at him with a look that frightens him but neither of them say a word to each other.

After a few minutes of trading looks at each other, Mia turns around, slowly. She bends over allowing Mike to get a really good look at her perfect brown ass. She spreads her legs a little exposing her vagina while picking up her pants. She stands up straight looking back at Mike. She sees he's rock hard, Mia smiles, shrugs her shoulders.

Mike watches her put her jeans back on. She turns to him and says, "Yeah, let's play rough."

Mia smiles one more time before leaving the bathroom. Mike hits the shower walls.

The next day Mike goes into the Cartier store. He scans the display case with tennis bracelets while a security guard keeps an eye on him. Mike points at a platinum and diamond encrusted bracelet. A female sales clerk unlocks the case taking the bracelet out. She sets down a black mat before gently placing the bracelet down. Mike picks it up, smiling at the diamonds sparkling in the overhead lights. He sits the bracelet back down and says, "I'll take it," the salesclerk smiles as Mike hands her his black card.

At home, Mia walks toward the front door carrying grocery bags while talking to Denise on the phone. The two laugh at what Mia did to Mike the night before. Denise says, "Cold water is child's play. I woulda threw hot grits on his ass." Mia laughs before responding, "OK Tyler Perry, I ain't trying to scar the man. I'm being petty, not violent." Denise smacks her teeth.

"Well you better than me." Mia chuckles, "This we both know." The women laugh again.

Once she enters, Mia sees the Cartier bag sitting in the middle of the foyer with flowers next to it. Mia stops walking, stares at the gesture.

"Girl you won't believe this." Anticipating what she's talking about, Denise asks, "What?" over and over.

Mia sits the grocery bags on the floor then takes the phone off her shoulder.

"Hold on, I'ma FaceTime you." Denise is excited.

"Oh shit, this must be good."

Mia FaceTimes Denise pointing the camera toward the flowers and Cartier bag. Denise reacts, "Damn them flowers, what's in the bag?"

Mia turns the camera back toward her as she responds to Denise.

"I don't know and I don't care." Denise isn't having that statement at all.

"Biiiiihhh! That's a Cartier bag!"

Mia shrugs her shoulders, she can care less what kind of bag it is let alone what's in it.

"So." Denise is dumbfounded, "What do you mean?"

Mia closes the door then picks up the groceries with her free hand and heads to the kitchen.

"Cause, I'm not gonna use or wear whatever it is. If I do, he wins." Denise continues to plead her case.

She can't understand why Mia doesn't see how she can use the gesture to her favor.

"Then sell it, return it. Do whatever and let's take a girl's trip on him."

Mia thinks about the idea as she puts the groceries away. Denise smiles at Mia seriously considering her idea. "Yeahhhhh, I see you thinkin' 'bout it. This time tomorrow we can be on an island with a few drinks in us, hopefully some dick in us too."

Mia's smile disappears faster than it appeared.

"See and that's where you lost me. Bye girl. Love me."

Mia's finger hovers over the end call button but Denise won't let her go. Denise protests, "You better not hang up on me. Mia!"

Mia ends the call smiling and shaking her head at Denise. She puts her phone down then walks back into the foyer. She looks down at the flowers and bag, then picks up the bag. Mia walks into the guest bedroom and opens the closet. The LV bag still sits in the corner untouched.

She holds the Cartier bag up to her face and talks baby talk to it.

"Here is your new home, and look, you already got a friend." Then she sits the bag next to the LV bag.

Exhaling from exhaustion mixed with frustration, Mia walks down the stairs stopping in front of the flowers. She picks them up reaching for the card, but she stops herself. She thinks. Smirks. Mia takes off all the petals from the roses then goes outside.

She places a trail of petals from the driveway to the door as well as leading to the foyer. Inside, she arranges the stems of the roses into a design. Then she lights a single candle and places it in the middle of the design. When she's done, she stands back, arms folded admiring her work. She wipes her hands then walks upstairs.

Later, Mike drives down the street of their neighborhood digging into his pant pocket. He retrieves his wedding ring, puts it on just as he arrives at his house. He smiles and chuckles when he sees the trail of roses.

"Now that's more like it."

Mike exits the car, waving at a neighbor across the street. The neighbor calls out, "I saw your wife put those down earlier. What's the occasion? Anniversary?" as he points at the rose petals. Mike shakes his head no.

"She did it just because." The man smiles nodding his head.

"Lucky man." Mike nods then turns back to looking at the flower petals. He says to himself, *Yes I am*. He then walks toward the front door. He opens the front door, the house is eerily quiet and dark. Only the flicker from the candle illuminates just enough light to allow Mike to follow the trail of rose petals. Then he stops in his tracks. A look of fear sweeps over his face.

Mike nervously looks around the house. He calls Mia's name, his voice shaking when it does. Mia doesn't answer, there's no sign she's even in the house. That makes Mike more fearful. Mike's eyes are fixed on Mia's design. With the rose stems Mia positioned them in a pentagon with the candle in the middle. Mike calls out, "MIA! THIS ISN'T FUNNY! ARE YOU IN HERE?" Mike listens, still no response. A gust of wind blows outside slamming the door shut. Mike jumps in horror, visually scared.

Upstairs in the bedroom, Mia covers her mouth as she laughs while she watches Mike's reaction from the security camera footage on her iPad. She watches Mike turn on the light. From her iPad, Mia shuts the lights off. Mike shutters when the lights go out. Mia, attempting to muffle her laughs, covers her mouth with both hands.

Mike turns on the light again and again, Mia shuts them off. Mike yells out, "STOP PLAYIN'. I GOT A GUN!". Mia laughs harder, putting the pillow over her face.

Mike turns the lights on one more time, anticipating they'll turn off again he doesn't take his hand off the switch. This time, Mia doesn't turn them back off. Mike inches toward the candle, scared. He picks it up then blows it out. He kicks the flower stems away, breaking up the pentagon design. He tosses the candle into the small decorative trash can beside the front door.

Mia continues to watch from her iPad as Mike cautiously walks up the stairs. Mia quickly puts the iPad away then turns off the lamp on the nightstand. She lays down pretending to be asleep. She can hear Mike walking toward the closed bedroom door. He puts his hand on the knob, slowly turning it, he whispers, "Mia?"

He listens, he can hear Mia breathing. He enters the bedroom turning the flashlight on his phone. Mike sees Mia fast asleep. He exhales a sigh of relief then turns off the flashlight.

Mike kicks off his shoes, undresses then quietly slides into bed trying not to disturb Mia, she doesn't move. Mike brings the comforter up to his chest as he lays on his back staring at the ceiling, wide awake.

He looks at Mia a few times before rolling over putting his back to her. A few moments later, Mike rolls over facing Mia's back. He thinks, then kisses her neck. Mia slightly moves, letting out a pleasing sigh. Mike smiles thinking he's been given the green light to go further. He gently places his hand on Mia's shoulder turning her on her back.

Mike looks down at her, she's still asleep. He then goes under the covers parting Mia's legs. Suddenly, Mia's body jolts up, her back arched as if she's possessed, she lets out a horrific sound. Scared out of his mind, Mike jumps up but his head is trapped under the comforter. He struggles to get out as Mia's body continues to jolt up and down.

Mike doesn't know how to get out, eventually he does, falling to the floor. He rolls over, putting his back against the wall and his fist balled up ready to throw a punch. He looks at the bed, Mia's body stops jolting up and down. She makes a whimper sound then rolls back over, sound asleep.

Mike sits completely still not sure if something else is going to happen. He sits against the wall trying to control his breathing. He knows Mia knows he's easily scared, still, this doesn't help him calm down. While Mike attempts to focus on his breathing, he can't help thinking why Mia is doing the things she's doing.

Did she not like the gift? Did he get her favorite flower wrong? Is that it? Is that why she's upset? Is she even upset? Regardless of the reason, Mia is obviously making Mike pay for a past or current indiscretion.

But what is it? What did he do now, he thinks to himself. Mike plays back the events from the past few weeks and to his recollection, she hasn't caught him cheating since the beard incident, so what could it be? Mike knows he's been smashing chicks like Wilt Chamberlain but does she know?

How could she know? He's been exceptionally careful to wash his dick and beard after every sneaky link.

He deletes his text history. All the nude pictures and videos are saved in a private folder on his phone that Mia doesn't know about. He was even smart enough to take Clive's advice and not save them to the cloud. So no, Mia can't know. As far as she should know, Mike has been the perfect husband.

Mike shakes off his thoughts as he slowly makes it to his feet. He stands next to the bed looking at his wife, unsure if he should get back into bed or go sleep in one of the other bedrooms. Dismissing that thought, Mike creeps back into the bed. The comforter is all over the place, covering half of Mia's semi-nude body.

Mike looks at the curvature of her thighs and butt licking his lips. He looks down at his boxers. Yep, hard again. Determined not to be outwitted by Mia, Mike reaches over attempting to touch Mia's thigh. She lets out a snort as if she knows he's getting too close. Mike jumps back, retracting his hand. He looks down at Mia then rolls over in defeat. With her back still to Mike, Mia opens her eyes, smiles then goes back to sleep.

Months later, Mike's behavior has improved slightly, it's evident to Mia because the gifts keep coming. She now knows, even when there's no hard evidence, when Mike's cheated and just how many times. The items in the guest bedroom closet are piling up and Mike is none the wiser.

Despite the couple having regularly scheduled date nights, taking trips and celebrating anniversaries, Mike has never inquired about any of the cheating gifts he's given

Mia. She's used or worn gifts from birthdays and Christmas but the ones in the guest bedroom closet have remained unopened.

It's not that Mike hasn't noticed he hasn't seen the gifts. He's refraining from asking about them in fear Mia is going to ask why he gave them to her and he'll have to be honest with what they both know he's been doing. In Mike's mind, it's better left unsaid.

He thinks if Mia does know he's cheating then she'd say something. If she doesn't then he'll stay the course and endure her antics. Mia on the other hand is unbothered and is fully invested in her plan of action convinced Mike will get the hint and change.

There are moments where she thinks she should just give in and reveal to Mike she knows what's been going on. If it weren't for Denise also being with the shits, Mia would have given up months ago. Despite the marital civil war being waged between the couple, from the outside, none of their friends know what's going on. Luckily for Mike he hasn't made Mia have to come out of character while around their friend group or in public.

Mia's noticed that Mike is less secretive but she and Denise have concluded that's only because he's gotten better at hiding what he's doing. However, Mike has been coming home and staying home more. The gifts are also less frequent, which to Mia means there is light at the end of the tunnel, she believes she can actually win. Furthermore, Mike has started sending *on my way* home texts, which is reassuring to Mia but still suspicious because his location is turned off more times than most and Mia can't determine if he's coming from work or a whore's house.

As per the advice of Denise, Mia has not been withholding sex from Mike but she has implemented using condoms. Mike fought it at first but due to his philandering, Mia has become a pretty good liar. When asked why she wanted to start using condoms, Mia told Mike that her period has been irregular. Since they both don't want to have kids, it was a safer bet. Mike countered with, "Com'on, my pull out game strong tho."

He's right. In their entire relationship the couple hasn't had any pregnancy scares but again, that was the lie. Mia is not going to risk her health while Mike is out in these streets waving his dick around like Thor's hammer. It didn't take much convincing to get Mike on board with the condoms.

Despite getting ass whenever he wants, he wasn't going to hold out on Mia. No, that would be too suspicious to her. Most men can't go too long without sex, every woman knows that. And if Mike managed to not make love to Mia for an extended amount of time, she would undoubtedly know he was getting it from somewhere else. Mike can't risk her spidey senses to go in that direction. However, Mia's gawk gawk 3000 has been reserved for special occasions.

Throughout it all, Mike is still seeing Dr. Phil keeping him and the men at the barber ship abreast of what's going on within the relationship, minus not getting frequent head.

Chapter 4

Today is a very special day, Mia's turning 40. The last 6 years have been a whirlwind both personally and professionally. Mia has expanded her salon, she now has 2 shops with the newest one being located on the eastside of Atlanta.

She's busier than ever which is good for her and Mike. Having to divide her time between two locations means working longer hours and only getting one day off a week. This leaves Mike free to link up with women hoping Mia is too busy to recognize. Unfortunately for him, he keeps buying her gifts. So even though she's busier, Mia still knows what's going on and she hasn't let up on making Mike pay for it.

The biggest thing for Mike is the food. It's gotten so bad that he's hired a chef to come to the home to meal prep for the week. Yes, it's a woman and yes, he's slept with her as well. Several times but Mike doesn't buy gifts each time.

But for the past few weeks Mia has been anxiously anticipating her 40th birthday. She just knows that Mike has something extravagant up his sleeve for her milestone birthday. But that will have to wait until later as Mia has opted to work on her special day.

Mia doesn't know but her main salon is decorated for a birthday. A large banner with the words HAPPY BIRTHDAY hangs from the ceiling. Various colors of balloons hang from the chairs as well as a huge balloon Arc sitting in the middle of the salon. Several of the salon stylists fuss around fixing and placing additional decor.

Denise pours mimosas in champagne flutes on a silver platter. One of the stylists peaks out of the window and sees Mia getting out of her car.

"She's coming! She's coming!" she announces.

Denise claps her hands, getting the women's attention. "OK ladies. It's time to get in formation!"

The ladies rush to the middle of the room standing in front of the balloon arch posing like Beyonce dancers. They wait. The salon door opens. Mia enters looking at her phone.

The women loudly scream, "SURPRISE!!" Mia jumps, dropping her phone with a scared look on her face.

The ladies clap and cheer. Mia finally realizes what's going on. She smiles to the women, "Awww stop, ya'll gonna make a boss bitch ugly cry up in here." The women laugh.

The women step to the side revealing the balloon arch.

Mia covers her mouth as tears of joy stream down her face. A stylist walks the silver platter of mimosas to Mia. She takes one, then the stylist passes the rest out.

Denise tells Mia they've canceled all the clients for the day. The food is catered and the mimosas are bottomless.

Denise and the other women raise their glasses in salute. "Happy 40th to a real one!" Denise toasts.

Mia smiles big. They all drink, someone turns on music and the party is underway. In the middle of the celebration, there's a knock at the door. The ladies turn their attention to the door, inquisitive. Mia goes to the door and opens it. An attractive man stands outside. He smiles a Colgate smile at Mia. She looks him up and down, unable to help noticing his locs draped over his broad shoulders and chiseled chin. He asks in a deep voice, "Are you Mia?"

She looks behind her at the women, some smiling big and admiring his attractiveness. Mia turns back to him and says, "Yes, but we're not taking any clients today. My apologies if you booked an appointment. Someone should have contacted you."

The man returns the smile. Takes Mia by the hand, looks her deep in the eyes and says in a low tone, "You are the client."

The Man enters the salon, tears off his clothes and he starts dancing raunchily on Mia. She smiles bashfully big, covering her face trying to stand still as the man dances on her. The other women hoot, holler and cheer while waving money in the air.

While Mia is busy trying not to enjoy eight pack abs and a bulging G-string being rubbed against her, Mike didn't remember today is her birthday. Instead, he's at lunch with two other lawyers from his firm.

Mike sits at a table in Buckhead with Corey, a 30-something and 40-year-old Craig, both realtors. Corey and Craig look over the menu, Mike swipes on another menu on his phone, Tinder. Craig and Corey make small talk with each other. Craig says, "I really got to close on this property or I can kiss that commission goodbye."

Corey looks at Mike, he's not paying attention but he speaks anyway.

"Maybe you should have Magic Mike talk to the buyers. If anyone can sell an unsellable house, it's Magic Mike."

Corey and Craig chuckle but Mike still doesn't respond. They stare at Mike then Craig yells across the table to get Mike's attention, "Yoooo Mike!" Mike looks up from his phone, he hides it under the table acting like he wasn't looking for a hookup.

"Yeah, yo, what's up?"

Craig and Corey give each other a look.

"What do you say? Come with me and help me put this thing to bed?" Craig asks.

Mike chuckles then goes back to swiping but responds to Craig's question, "I wouldn't do it for you when we worked for the same company, so I damn sure ain't gonna help my competition."

"Ahh com'on dude, help me out. I would help you out. We're boys. There's no "I" in team." Craig pleads. "There isn't. But there's an "I" in win!" Corey scoffs, "Oh he think he Jordan now."

Mike chuckles, Craig waves Mike off just as a young looking waitress makes her way to their table. She stands behind Mike on his left shoulder. She looks down at his phone then clears her throat.

Mike slightly jumps then puts the phone face down on the table and gives the waitress his attention, more so her body. She tells the men her name is Nicole and Nicole is a fun size light skinned woman with creole features. Mike checks her out. Ass is a nine, chest is a ten, waist is small and she's cute. Much too cute to be waiting tables for a bunch of corporate people in Atlanta.

Nicole gives the men her server spin then asks if they want to start off with something from the bar. Corey orders a double gin and tonic. Craig gives him shit for drinking on the job but Corey decides he's not going back into the office today. Craig shares his sentiment and joins in with ordering the same. Nicole then turns her attention to Mike. "Anything for you sir?", she asks with a very inviting smile.

Before Mike could answer, his phone chimes. He has a Tinder match but he ignores it because Nicole is staring into his soul or at least that's Mike's embarrassment taking over him. He finally says, "I'll have a Jameson and Ginger. Ginger ale, not ginger beer."

Nicole nods then turns to walk away. She doesn't get far before Craig belts out to keep the drinks coming. Nicole nods again, "Yes sir." Craig winks at her, Mike sees.

Seeing Craig is interested in Nicole, he interrupts her attention from him by asking, "Where is the restroom?"

Nicole points to an area just past the bar. Mike thanks her, Craig watches her hips sway as she walks away. Corey, watching the exchange says, "I saw that?" Craig doesn't deny he was looking.

"Did you see that ass though? I wonder if she got an only fans." Corey shakes his head as he replies, "If she did, I doubt she'd be working here." Craig lets out an oooooowwweee, "The things I have planned for her would put her in the top 5%. Watch out Black Chyna!"

The men laugh as Mike gets up and heads in the direction of the bathroom.

At the stall, Mike unzips his pants and takes a picture. He texts on his phone with a smile on his face, hits send and exits the stall. He washes his hands while checking himself out. He wipes his hands with a paper towel as he exits the bathroom. While exiting the restroom, Mike is too busy looking down wiping his hands to see Nicole coming in his direction. She sees he's preoccupied so she steps in his path. The two bump into each other, exactly what Nicole was hoping for. Mike doesn't look up, "My apologies. Excuse me." Nicole smiles.

Mike attempts to step around her. Nicole steps in his way again. This time, Mike looks up.

"Sorry."

Nicole looks at Mike with a smile. She swipes her hand across Mike's face. Mike looks confused.

"Uhh OK, not sure what that was." Nicole swipes across his face again.

"I swiped right on you."

The moment he got the Tinder reference, Nicole leans in close to Mike's ear. She whispers, "And I promise you, I'm more fun."

Nicole steps back. She looks around before taking out her phone. She presses send. Then walks away. Mike watches Nicole walk away. His phone chimes.

Mike looks at it and sees Nicole air dropped her phone number. He smiles.

The day has quickly turned into night. Mia and Denise sit in the salon chairs looking happy but tired as they sip mimosas. Mia looks over at Denise. "Thank you girl. I really needed some fun like that." Denise gives Mia a sneaky look, "The party, or that big ol' blickey that dancer was pressing all up on yo butt?"

Mia is smiling covering her face. Denise continues teasing, "Mmmm hmmm, I saw you poking for a better feel."

Mia swats at Denise.

"Shut up, you tryna get me in trouble."

Denise gets up, walks to the table pouring more champagne in her glass, continuing talking, "Shiiiit, if you can forgive Mike all those times, he could forgive you once."

Mia looks sad. Denise turns around to see Mia's head down. Immediately she realizes the error in her comment.

"You know what I mean." Mia looks at Denise, "You just suggested I cheat on my husband."

Denise makes it back to the chair beside Mia trying to recover from what she just said. Denise isn't sorry for saying what she said. She feels bad that Mia took it the wrong way. Denise tries to explain to Mia what she's been saying the past six years. If Mike is going to play the field then Mia should get into the game too.

Mia explains she's not like that. Just because Mike is doing it doesn't make it right. She believes it's worse when a woman cheats on her significant other. Men are built to cheat, they can't help it. But women are to hold themselves to a higher standard. Even if she doesn't believe everything she just said, it brings Mia some sort of peace. Being petty is one thing, but cheating is the line she doesn't cross.

Denise, however, lives by the standards of the old testament, an eye for an eye. "I build like these niggas, I do what they do. And I'd sleep right next to my cheatin' ass husband with a smile on my face with another man's dick on my breath."

Mia bursts into laughter, Denise joins in but they both know she's serious. Mia jokes, "Oh My god you're a mess."

"Yep and I make one too."

Mia gets up from the chair, grabs a big balloon and her purse, that's her cue to go. Tipsy off a day of drinking and horny from the male stripper, Mia is ready for the second part of her birthday which she is convinced is going to be epic.

Before she leaves, Denise tells Mia to think about what she said but again, Mia rejects the notion. Denise comes back with, "If being with another man is the issue, then there's always a woman." Denise raises an eyebrow.

Mia turns around giving Denise a look, "I'm just sayin', eatin' ain't cheatin.'"

Mia laughs again then the two exchange I love you's before Mia stumbles out of the salon.

While Mia reaches her car headed for the home she shares with Mike, Mike exits the elevator doors of a condo. He walks down the hallway then stops in front of an apartment door. He looks at his text message, reads the number on the door before putting his phone away and knocking. The door opens revealing Nicole in her bra and panties. She has a drink in her hand.

"Come in."

Nicole closes the door behind Mike. He walks in, looking around. Then he faces Nicole. She hands him the drink and says, "Jameson and Ginger. Ginger ale, not Ginger beer." Mike takes the drink smiling, "I see what you did there?" Nicole seductively poses against the wall, asking, "What else do you see?"

Nicole licks her lips. Mike looks Nicole up and down before saying, "A whole lotta things I like." Nicole kisses Mike. Then takes him by the hand.

"Com'on, let me feed you."

Mike passes on the offer stating he's still full from the lunch he had earlier. Nicole looks at him, "Who said anything about food?" Nicole walks toward a bedroom. Mike's eyes grow wide. He chugs the drink, then kicks off his shoes as he follows Nicole.

Meanwhile, Mia pulls into the driveway. From inside the car she looks at the house. It's dark as if no one is home and she doesn't see Mike's car. She chalks it up to him, parking in the garage. And the dark house? A surprise party, that's why Denise kept her at the salon so long, to give Mike time to prepare. *She ain't slick,* Mia said smiling to herself.

Mia exits the car carrying the balloons, walks toward the house. She punches in the door code. She enters anticipating her second surprise of the day, but it doesn't happen. Confused, she calls for Mike.

No answer. She looks behind her toward the street. Hmm, no cars. Maybe there isn't a party. But if there isn't, where is Mike?

Mia calls for him again.

"Baby please don't jump out and try to scare me. I'm from Maryland. When we get scared we get the swingin'." Mia listens.

She puts her purse on an end table, turns on the light, and looks around. The house is completely empty. She takes out her phone, dials Mike.

Unbeknownst to Mia, the real party is going on right now at Nicole's condo. Music plays and on the floor, Mike's phone sits on top of his shirt vibrating. The headboard hits the wall, Nicole's moans get more intense each time Mike slaps her ass. She and Mike engage in talking dirty to each other. Nicole asks, "You like how that sounds? You like that macaroni and cheese sound baby?"

SLAP! Mike admits he loves it. Nicole continues, "You gonna get seconds? Huh, you want seconds of this macaroni baby?" SLAP! Mike yells out

"Hell yeah!"

Left standing in the middle of the foyer, Mia listens as she gets Mike's voicemail. She looks at the phone in disbelief before hanging up. She looks at the time. 8:4 7p.m. Before getting upset and thinking the worst, Mia tries to justify Mike's absence. Maybe he got held up with a buyer. Maybe he lost track of time. Maybe he's out shopping for a last-minute gift.

Any scenario sounds better than thinking Mike forgot her birthday, or worse yet, he was with another woman when he should be with her, of all days, especially today.

Mia closes the door and heads upstairs hoping there's a gift, card, balloon or smoke signal to reassure her that Mike remembered her day. After all, he hasn't called her once today. Mia now remembers Mike left this morning without wishing her a happy birthday. They had normal conversation like any other day. At first, Mia thought Mike was pretending not to remember because he had something big up his sleeve. But the later and later it gets, Mia begins to realize he might've actually forgotten.

Back in Nicole's bedroom, Mike lays on his back catching his breath. Nicole sits Indian style rolling a blunt. She lights it, takes a long drag blowing out a cloud of smoke. She passes it to Mike. He declines, making Nicole give him a *really* look.

"Don't be scared, I won't tell anyone. I know all you guys at least smoke."

Mike is surprised at Nicole's assumption of his profession. He looks at her as he hits the blunt.

"How'd you know?" Nicole lays on Mike's chest, "Only two types of men wearing suits come into a restaurant in the middle of the day and drink like ya'll did. Entrepreneurs and finance guys." Mike chuckles, "Maybe I'm a finance guy."

Nicole takes the blunt, inhales while shaking her head no, "If you were, the coke woulda came out by now."

The two laugh but it's short lived. Mike quickly sits up when he hears a door close. A female voice calls for Nicole. She tells the voice she's in the room.

Mike gets nervous. He's heard stories about women setting up men. They fuck them then rob them. He's scared now, he looks at the window. The view of the city reminds him of what floor he's on so jumping out of the window is out of the question. Nicole sees Mike's uneasiness, she tries to calm him down.

"Relax baby, that's just my girlfriend."

At the sound of that, Mike's emotions are mixed with excitement and fear. What kinda girlfriend does Nicole have? Is she a homegirl type of girlfriend or a lover? Mike jumps out of bed in his fighting stance.

Again, Nicole tries to reassure Mike there's nothing to worry about. The door opens. Alisha, an equally pretty 20 something rocking natural hair enters the bedroom. She's talking about her day and doesn't see Mike standing in the corner like a fighter waiting for the bell. She begins to undress as she speaks, "Sorry I'm late. My professor kept me after class talking 'bout I'm not applying myself enough."

Nicole gives Alisha the blunt. She takes a long drag then she sees the confused look on Mike's face. She smiles at him.

"Hey."

Mike nods his head, still unsure if everything is cool. "Sup." Alisha goes back to her initial conversation.

"I think he's just being a hard ass and for no reason at all. I can't wait til this semester is over."

Mike looks at Nicole then back at Alisha, he can't believe what's happening. Now naked, Alisha passes the blunt to Mike. He hesitates before taking it. He takes it and Alisha gets in the bed with Nicole. Mike's eyes are wide as he coughs blowing out the smoke. Alisha looks at him.

"So, you ready for seconds?" Nicole answers for him, "Oh girl , he already had seconds."

"Well then. Dessert it is."

Alisha throws back the covers, inviting Mike in bed. Reluctantly he moves toward the bed. Alisha and Nicole giggle at his apprehension. Finally Mike gets in bed. Alisha wastes no time putting Mike into her mouth. Mike's eyes roll in the back of his head, he leans back on the pillow calling to God. Nicole smiles, "I told you she was cool."

Mike nods between moaning. Nicole puts the blunt in her mouth then sits on Mike's face. A reminder flashes on Mike's screen: MIA'S BIRTHDAY TODAY.

Mia, dressed in an evening gown anticipating going to a private airport to be flown somewhere exotic or at least a nice dinner, quickly paces around the bedroom, holding her phone, talking to herself out loud. *Oh he must be out his goddamn mind! He gonna come in late on my birthday.*

She stops to look in the mirror and have a conversation with her reflection.

"Yes bitch! He doing this on your birthday! He got us fucked all the way up!" She continues pacing and talking. "See! See! You try to be nice, that don't work. You try being mean, that don't work. You give a nigga an inch, he takes the whole damn state!"

Mia stops pacing. Thinks. She looks towards their shared closet. Mia snatches open the walk-in closet door. She looks at Mike's side of the closet.

"I got something for his ass. I'ma go Angela Bassett, waiting to exhale on all his shit."

Mia starts snatching clothes off the hangers like a mad woman. Her pristine hairdo flings around with every movement. Sweat beads in her forehead. She stops, thinks. "Or maybe I just wait for him to bop his happy ass in this house and go Angela Bassett What's Love Got To Do With It limo scene on his ass."

Mia throws wild punches in the air. She stops. Thinks again coming up with a new way to get the ultimate payback when Mike decides to come home.

"Or maybe I go evil Angela Bassett, A Thin Line Between Love & Hate and kill'em. Yeah, he's gonna die. He's gonna die tonight."

Mia flops down on the bed, sobbing. She hears Denise's voice in her head encouraging her to have a little fun since Mike continues to do his own thing. Mia looks at her reflection in the tall mirror then smirks. She leaps to her feet leaving the room.

She heads for the guest bedroom and stands in front of the closet for a minute. Her chest rises and falls with each frustrated breath. She shifts back and forth contemplating what she should do next. Then she does it. Mia opens the guest bedroom closet door. It's full of unopened gifts. Mia stands in awe looking at everything.

Mia is amazed at the sheer volume of the gifts. In the beginning she neatly placed the gifts in the closet. But over time she started just tossing them in not caring about the placement. Now, the closet looks like a crowded attic that no one's been in for years. She continues talking to herself, "All this stuff. All these women. All these years. Well fuck that. New year, new me dammit!"

Mia grabs the first gift she sees and tears it open. It's a blue alligator skin Brahmin purse. She tosses it on the bed then reaches for another one. She grabs a small gift bag and takes out a Tiffany blue box. She opens it and stares at a beautiful diamond and platinum necklace. Then she grabs another gift, it's a black Tom Ford cocktail dress. Then another gift, red bottom shoes.

After an hour, Mia opens all the gifts. The closet and part of the room is littered with bags, tissue paper and boxes resembling the Christmas morning every child, or sugar baby, dreams of. She looks at all the items neatly placed on the bed. She looks over everything then grabs one of the 7 pairs of shoes, a dress, bracelet, earrings and the Tiffany necklace before leaving the room.

Standing in front of the bathroom mirror in a black sheer lace bra and panties set, Mia applies makeup and lipstick, then she fixes her hair doing it in a new style. She straightens it then slightly curls it at the ends. Once she's satisfied with her look she walks back into the bedroom.

On the bed, a dress is neatly laid out with the necklace and other jewelry from Mike. Everything is laid out the way kids do the night before the first day of school. At the foot of the bed are a pair of red bottom shoes.

Mia takes a deep breath, nods her head then begins to get dressed. Afterwards, she stands in front of a full-length mirror looking like she's ready for someone's red carpet. She hasn't looked this good in years. Mike may be an inconsiderate asshole and a cheat, but goddamn he knows what Mia likes. The idea that another woman helped him do the shopping crept into Mia's mind but she quickly dismissed the thought.

Mia struts down the stairs into the foyer symbolically wearing the first LV purse Mike had gotten her when the gifts started. Tonight marks the first night of what Mia is going to do going forward. She stands in front of the door, waiting, hoping one last time that Mike would walk through the door. At this point she doesn't even want an explanation, she just wants to spend her birthday with her husband.

But the door doesn't open. After a while, Mia opens the front door. Mia stands in the doorway looking down both ends of the street. No sign of Mike's car driving toward the house. She exhales then closes the door.

Mia speeds down the street blasting music. The International Players Anthem blares from the speakers, "Don't do it. Reconsider. Read some literature on the subject."

Mia quickly changes the radio station. The City Girl's F-Boy free plays. "Yeeeeahhhhh," Mia shouts as she weaves in and out of traffic on the highway. She sings along dancing to the music.

Mia arrives at a lounge. The valet attendant opens her door helping her out of the car. She smiles and thanks him then walks toward the large black bouncer managing a long line behind the velvet rope. A woman sees Mia walking to the front and shouts out, "The line is back there."

Mia smiles at the woman as she takes 2 one-hundred-dollar bills from her purse. She turns to the bouncer giving him the money. He looks at her with a smile as he steps aside to let Mia in. Before she opens the door she turns back to the bouncer. She points to the young woman and tells him, "Make sure she doesn't get in." Then she gives him another hundred dollars.

"Yes ma'am. Enjoy yourself," he says.

"I intend to."

Mia walks through a crowded lounge feeling nervous inside but her head is held high. Her outward confidence is on 100. The music is loud and it's dimly lit. A couple talks to each other as Mia passes them. The man looks at Mia's butt. His woman, same age as Mia but doesn't look as good, sees him staring. She smacks him upside the head and they begin arguing as she pulls him away.

Mia stops walking and looks around the lounge. She sees several people popping bottles in the VIP section, some standing on couches. True Atlanta shit. Mia takes a seat at the bar.

Beside her are a group of young women celebrating loudly. Toya, a black woman throws money in the air as a woman twerks in front of them. She shakes her head then looks toward the bar and finds an open seat.

Mia takes a seat at the bar.

Beside her are a group of young women celebrating loudly. Toya, a black woman who turned 30 today, wears a gold crown and a birthday sash with money pinned all over it. The bartender puts down a bunch of shots in front of the women. Mia gets the bartender's attention.

"Excuse me." The bartender stops in front of Mia leaning over the bar trying to talk over the music.

"What can I get you?"

Mia thinks then looks over at the birthday girl. She says, "I'll have two of what they're having." The bartender smiles, "Yes ma'am." The Bartender walks away.

Mia looks at the party girls. She taps Toya on the shoulder. Toya turns around. Mia leans forward and wishes her a happy birthday. Excited, Toya thanks Mia with a hug. Then Mia informs Toya it's also her birthday. Toya lets out a scream and tells her friends, "Ayyyyye!! Ya'll it's her birthday too!" Her friends cheer for Mia.

Toya continues shouting over the music talking to Mia. "It's my dirty thirty! What about you?"

Mia struggles to say she's forty. "Ummm, umm, it's my fuck it forties."

Toya checks out Mia's ass making Mia slightly uncomfortable fearing other people would look too. "Thass wassup!! You look so damn good to be 40. You got a Meg the Stallion booty. Where'd you go? Miami or the DR?"

Mia is slightly insulted at Toya suggesting she's gotten plastic surgery but then again, these are the times we live in. Mia simply replies with, "What? No, this is just cornbread and mamba sauce." Toya screams, "Daaaaaayum!!!"

The Bartender drops off Mia's drinks. Toya suggests they all do a shot together. Mia, Toya and the other women pick up their drinks. Toya talks even louder, getting the attention of people at the bar and nearby in the lounge. "Here's to being a bad bitch at 30 and a queen at 40!" Mia replies with an enthusiastic, "Hell yeah!"

The group of women scream HAPPY BIRTHDAY!!! Then they all take their shots.

Toya, clearly inebriated, looks down at her birthday sash and offers it to Mia. Mia, thinking the sash is a bit much, plays it off by being modest. She politely declines but Toya insists as she takes it off and puts it around Mia ignoring her saying no. Toya demands.

"Take it! It might attract some attention. Niggas love buying birthday girls drinks."

Toya squints as she tries to adjust the sash on Mia. Mia thanks her with a smile and the women hug again. Toya tells Mia to enjoy her night then she walks away with her group of friends. Mia looks down at the sash realizing Toya's money is still attached to it.

Mia calls for Toya. One of her friends hears and turns a stumbling Toya around.

"At least lemme give you your money." Toya waves.

"It's OK. I'm fuckin a dude with a whole wife. He gives me more than enough money to keep my mouth shut and full." Toya winks then walks away.

Toya's admission worries Mia. Did she just say she's messing with a married man? Could it be her husband? Could she be one of the reasons why Mike's given her a gift? Looking at Toya she admits that she's the type of woman Mike would go for. Young, dumb and is probably sleeping on an air mattress somewhere. Her curiosity and anxiety are getting the best of her and if she's going to go on with the night, she has to know for sure.

She fights her way through the crowd and finds Toya in the VIP section just as a waitress brings over a bottle with sparklers. Mia leans over the rope and asks Toya, "Is his name Mike? He in real estate." Toya and her friends laugh then she says, "Real estate? Oh no! I don't mess with square dudes. Only ball players, rappers and trappers."

Mia breathes a sigh of relief. She turns around facing the bar and takes her second shot. She signals the bartender to bring her two more. The Bartender nods. Mia bops to the music as she checks her messages. None from Mike. Then she tells herself *Fuck this. Just have fun girl, have fun. It's your day.* She puts her phone back in her purse.

Behind her a strong voice says, "Excuse me, is this seat taken?"

Mia turns around to see Terry standing beside her. She slowly looks him up and down. She focuses on his lips. Jawline. His muscular arms. His eyes. She's completely smitten. Terry watches her stare at him with her mouth agape.

"Uhhh, hello. Are you OK?"

Mia still doesn't answer. She remembers the face that flashed in her head so long ago when she pleasured herself and it looks at lot like this one. But how could that be? Mia can hear her heartbeat. The man's words sound muffled and her head is spinning. What the hell did she drink? Maybe she's drunk off the scent of his cologne.

He tries to get her attention again, "Hellllloooooo!"

The man waves his hand in front of Mia's face. She snaps out of it. Her eyes immediately get big. She looks down at her lap. She covers her mouth.

"Shit. Umm." He chuckles.

"You good? Can I sit down?"

Mia jumps from her seat. The man jumps back confused. Mia looks at him, shaking.

"Uhhhh. I'll be right back."

Mia rushes off leaving her phone and purse on the bar. The man watches her rush off, he notices her purse and tries to call after her but Mia doesn't hear him. He sits down.

Mia rushes into the bathroom stall pulling her panties down but they get caught on the heel. She fights with it a second while trying to keep her balance. Finally she gets them off. She examines them, they're wet. Like wet wet. She talks to herself, Ain't no way he got me like this. I don't even know him. How old is that line anyway?" She mocks the man's line, "Excuse me. Is anyone sitting here?" She balls up her panties looking for somewhere to put them. She thinks, noticing she doesn't have her purse or her phone.

She stomps like a toddler thinking the strange man who got her kitty throbbing is going to run off with her stuff. Mia sighs then stuffs her panties in her dress in the middle of her breasts. She then slightly opens the stall door. Peaks out. The bathroom is empty. She hurries out, rushes to the sink and washes her hands. Mia looks at herself in the mirror. She turns to the left. Then the right while staring at her chest. She pats her chest. Confident the panties aren't causing a bulge in her bra she leaves the bathroom.

Mia walks back to the bar. The man is still standing there when she comes back. Mia sees her purse and phone still sitting on top of the bar. She celebrates inside then rushes over to it. "Yes! Yes! Yes! It's still here!"

Mia picks up the purse, hugs it. The man looks over at her and says, "Yeah. A few people tried to walk off with it, but I fought them off. I think my heroics deserve a drink."

Mia looks at him. They make eye contact for the first time. She smiles, he smirks. Mia points to her sash, flirting she says, "Do you see this?" He replies.

"I do. Happy birthday."

"Thank you. And this means you're supposed to buy me a drink, not the other way around."

The man leans back looking at Mia with a raised eyebrow. He asks if it wasn't her birthday would she buy him a drink. Mia says yes. He's surprised.

"Really? You'd buy a man a drink?"

Now Mia's surprised at his question. She giggles before responding.

"Why not? I believe chivalry goes both ways."

The man smiles, he likes her response. The two look at each other in silence for a minute before Mia snaps out of her trance.

"Would you please sit down, my neck hurts from looking up at you. How tall are you?"

He obliges sitting in the chair next to Mia, closely then he answers the question that everyone asks him.

"6'6. Yes, I played basketball, professionally. I'm retired now."

Mia and the man exchange in harmful conversation about how retirement is treating him. He states that he doesn't do the whole golf thing, instead he plays racquetball. He says he likes to stay active and judging by his physique, Mia thinks he's doing a great job staying in shape.

"I pretty much stay in the country club and the studio. Podcasting, not rapping."

Mia's relieved she's not talking to an old wanna be rapper. If she was, she'd kindly show him to Toya's VIP section. He laughs at her response before saying, "You're funny. And incredibly sexy." Mia bashfully smiles, looking away.

She looks back at him, thanks him. He looks down at her ring finger. Mia can see a slight disappointing look on his face as he tries to hide it.

"Your husband is a lucky man."

His comment catches Mia off guard. She looks down at her ring, then back at Terry.

"You saw that huh?"

"Yes, when I first walked over."

Mia looks at him matter of factly.

"And you flirted with me anyway? Why?"

He holds up his left hand, showing the wedding band on his ring finger. Mia looks at his finger. Scoffs. He turns his face up.

"What's wrong?"

Mia looks at Terry, cups his cheek and leans forward. "This would have been so much easier if you were single. I know how it feels to be cheated on and I can't do that to your wife."

Mia puts some cash on the bar then gets up to leave. He takes her hand. Mia stops, looks at him.

"My wife and I have an understanding."

Mia gives him a look, her face says, *do you think I'm a fool?* He notices then pulls out his phone.

"Don't believe me? Call her, right now." He hands Mia the phone. She pushes it away.

"I'm not calling your wife." He shrugs.

"I'm just trying to put your mind at ease."

Mia's mouth opens as if she wants to say something but she doesn't. The man stands. He slowly gets close to Mia's ear. She smells his neck, closes her eyes enjoying the scent.

He whispers, "I'm Terry by the way."

Chapter 4

Nicole and Alisha sleep cuddled with each other. The sun peaks through the windows shining bright on Mike's face. He squints his eyes as he wakes up. He slowly sits up, stretches then looks over at Nicole and Alisha. Then it hits him.

"Oh shit! I slept here?!"

Mike jumps out of bed, tripping over Alisha's shoes. He frantically searches for his phone and finds it. He looks at the screen, sees the several missed calls from Mia as well as the birthday reminder. He yells out, "FUCK!" Nicole talks in her sleep.

"You ready to go again baby?" Mike ignores her question as he dresses quickly and darts out of the condo.

Mia is about to have a similar reaction as Mike. A shirtless Terry sits on the edge of the bed watching Mia sleep peacefully. Her phone alarm goes off. Mia reaches over to hit it. It falls on the floor, the alarm stops. Terry wishes Mia a good morning. Mia rolls over smiling, opening her eyes. She sees Terry, then sits up quickly covering herself and pleading, "Oh no, no, no, no, no! We didn't." Mia looks under the covers, then to Terry.

"Please tell me we didn't." Terry forces a smile, unsure how to read Mia's reaction to her being naked under a set of 800 thread count hotel sheets.

"We did."

Mia leaps out of the bed with the sheet wrapped around her looking around the room for her clothes, hurling questions at a seemingly relaxed Terry.

"Why'd you let me fall asleep? My husband is going to kill me. Oh my god! Oh my god!"

Terry, calmly, hands Mia some of her items laughing when she snatches them away putting them back on.

"It's not funny! And why are you still naked! Put some clothes on." Mia looks down at Terry's dick.

She gasps clenching her imaginary pearls. He looks at him asking, "Is that morning wood?" Confidently Terry responds, "Nope."

Mia flops down on the bed, covering her face with her hands.

"I shouldn't have done this. I shoulda listen to 3 stacks. He said to reconsider."

Mia drops her hands, lifting her head quickly with scared wide eyes.

"Please tell me we used a condom." Terry looks away.

With that gesture, Mia got her answer. She leaps to her feet. She grabs her shoes off the floor. Terry tries to comfort her but she shields herself.

"Don't!"

Terry goes to say something but she holds her hand up and he stops talking. Mia breathes. Calms herself down.

"It's not your fault but I gotta go, like now!"

Mia heads for the door but immediately stops when she hears Terry ask if he can text her later. Mia quickly turns around, a serious look on her face. She points and walks slowly toward Terry.

"No! Don't call me, text me, don't slide in my DM's, send me a message by pigeon, nothing!"

Mia stops when her finger hits Terry's chest. He throws his hands up in surrender, smiling.

"OK got it. No contact. Heard."

"Good." Mia looks down, gasps, pouts.

"Okaaaayy. Maybe wait a few days. If you don't see my picture on the news, then I'm still alive."

Mia quickly kisses Terry, he's surprised. Mia darts out of the room.

Mia anxiously waits for the elevator doors to open. He fidgets occasionally looking around at the other closed hotel room doors to see if anyone is going to come out. DING! Finally the doors open and Mia rushes in. She presses the lobby button several times in attempts to close the door before anyone else can enter the elevator.

The doors close and Mia becomes mortified to see her reflection in the glass door. Her dress is on backwards and her shoes are on the wrong feet. She desperately wiggles out of the dress using the sides of the elevator walls to keep her balance. She watches the numbers descend hoping they don't stop on another floor.

She looks out of the doors to see if anyone is staring up at the elevator before she turns the dress right side up, then jumps into it. She switches her shoes then using her reflection, she fixes her hair. She gathers herself, clenches her purse and takes a deep breath just as the elevator reaches the lobby.

The posh hotel lobby is bustling with people going on with their day. Mia puts her hair behind her ear before exiting the elevator. She makes her way through the lobby trying to act inconspicuous. The front door seems like a mile away and her heels clack loudly furthering Mia's nervousness. Finally she can see the valet stand, she's almost home free without anyone stopping her. The worst thing that can happen is someone calling her name, then she'll be busted. But she thinks God isn't that cruel.

The automatic doors open and Mia steps out shielding herself from the blinding bright sun. The valet looks at Mia, nods then takes off running. Mia nervously taps her purse as she waits for her car to arrive. She continues to look around but sure to avoid eye contact with anyone.

In Mia's mind it's taking an eternity to get her car, in actuality it's only been a few seconds. She checks her watch but hears the sound of a car coming around the corner. She looks up, her eyes light up, it's her car. She steps out in front of it making the valet slam on the brakes to avoid hitting her.

She snatches open the driver side door before the valet could open it. To his surprise she yanks him out of the car. She tosses a few dollars at him then jumps in the car speeding off like a bat out of hell. The valet picks the money off the ground before it could blow away in the wind. He looks at Mia's taillights shaking his head.

"Yeah, she cheated on somebody last night."

Speeding, Mia smacks her forehead over and over again. How could she be so stupid. Not only did she cheat but she didn't come home last night. Hell, even Mike comes home. To make matters worse, he wakes up before she does so at this point he knows she's not there. She checks her phone. No missed calls. No texts from Mike.

That comes off as strange to her. If he woke up and she wasn't there, why wouldn't he at least call to find out if she's OK. Mia begins to think Mike doesn't care about her. She fights back the tears and says fuck it. Just in case Mike is awake and waiting for her, she'll have her story straight.

She uses her car's handsfree option to call Denise. The phone rings. And rings. And rings. Finally Denise picks up. "What's up girl?"

Mia talks just as fast as she's driving.

"Hey, did Mike call you this morning?" Denise makes a gagging sound.

"Why would he call me?" Mia thinks for a second, maybe Mike doesn't know.

"In case he does, or if it comes up later, I slept at your house last night OK?"

Denise screams with excitement.

"Good for you. I wanna know all the details." Mia hurries Denise off the phone, "OK, OK. I'll tell you later. Bye!" Denise laughs and teases, "Bye heaux."

Mia hangs the phone up feeling bad.

She convinces herself that it doesn't matter now, what's done is done. She just can't get caught. Mia fears what Mike would do to her if he found out she let some strange man shoot up her club last night.

She shutters with fear just thinking about it. But then again, maybe it would be good for him to see how it feels.

Her emotions flip flop from feeling guilty to feeling no remorse at all. On one hand she thinks she's just as bad as Mike but on the other hand, he did miss her birthday and drastic times calls for drastic measures. Mia tries to clear her mind and not let her imagination run away on its own. She takes a few deep breaths, grips the wheel tight and tries to focus on not getting a speeding ticket.

As her mind becomes calm, images of sex with Terry flashes in her mind making her wet again. She remembers how his tongue felt between her legs. His strong large basketball player hands gripping her ass when he picked her up putting her on his shoulders.

Her nipples get hard thinking about the force of each thrust when Terry bent her over as well as the surprise and pleasure she experienced when he massaged her butthole.

That was something new, something Mike had never done, intentionally or by accident but she liked it, a lot! Terry did a lot of things she liked, maybe a lot of those things were things she's been missing. She couldn't help thinking if what he told her was true.

Did he and his wife have an understanding? Is that what people out here are doing nowadays? Is no one monogamous anymore? Is she now one of those people? So many thoughts flood Mia's mind about Mike that it's hard to concentrate. It's like the devil is on one shoulder and an angel on the other, and the angel is judging the hell out of her.

Is she going to see Terry again? Of course she is the devil says. Of course not, the angel says. Should she come clean to Mike? The angel and the devil agree that she shouldn't, that'll be the fastest way to the upper room. She had such a great time last night and Mike was out obviously having the time of his life, good enough to miss her birthday. So should she consider having an understanding with Mike? The devil absolutely agrees, but the angel reminds Mia of the commitment she made to God and her family.

But how bad could it be? It's not like she wants to leave Mike for Terry, or does she? No, no, no, that's foolish. It's just sex...maybe a little more than sex. Terry made her feel the way Mike used to make her feel. It's not just that Terry wanted her body, he appreciated her giving it to him. He showed that with every touch. Every kiss. Every thrust.

Mike has her heart but she could share her body if it means they're both getting what they want. Right?

Meanwhile, Mike is out trying to plan his damage control. Ugh, so many questions to be answered. But when?

Meanwhile, Mike is out trying to plan his damage control. He exits a cake shop with a cake in his hand walking to his car as he talks on the phone with Craig.

"OK, she didn't call and that could mean she didn't wake up yet. I just gotta get home before she does." Craig agrees.

"OK, good idea. If she wakes up before you get there and calls, I'll tell her you slept here and your phone died."

Mike reaches the car and balances the cake in one hand, his phone on his opposite shoulder trying to open the door.

"My guy! Thanks."

"I got you bruh."

Happy he's secured his alibi, Mike hangs up and gets into the car peeling off.

Mia speeds down the street almost hitting a woman walking her dog as she crosses the street. She turns into the driveway, hitting the closed garage door. She checks herself in the rearview mirror then gets out of the car.

The Dog Walking Woman walks by giving Mia an evil look. Mia waves and gives her a sincere apology while hurrying toward her house. The Dog Walking Woman gives Mia the finger. Mia waves her off then enters the house cautiously.

She peaks around the door calling for Mike. She listens but he doesn't respond. The house is too quiet for anyone to be home. Suspecting the coast is clear, Mia enters the house closing the door and running from room to room on the bottom level looking for Mike. It's clear, he isn't home. Whew!

Mia rushes into the bedroom, kicking off her shoes and tearing off her clothes. She frantically puts on a shirt and leggings. Then she scrubs off her makeup.

Mia checks herself out in the mirror. Then messes up her hair. She looks around the room and sees the bed is made. Not just made but it looks exactly the way it did when she made it up yesterday. Mike never makes up the bed. She decides to go look in the guest bedroom. It's still in disarray from her frantic episode last night.

She stands in the middle of the room with her hands on her hips thinking. Did Mike spend the night out? The thought of that being a possibility pisses Mia off.

"That son of a bitch!" she yells out.

Mia decides she'll get mad later, right now she has to clean up the room. At first she folds the bags neatly to organize everything back in the closet. Then she remembers Mike never comes into the room. She chooses to just throw things back in any bag just to get it up and she shoves everything back in the closet.

She runs out of the guest bedroom and down the stairs straight into the kitchen. She takes out a cast iron frying pan, throws some oil in it, spilling some on the stove in the process. She turns on the gas.

She carelessly tosses a few pieces of bacon in the pan then drops two eggs when she snatches the carton from the fridge. She feels herself sweating again. She looks toward the garage door listening, Mike isn't home yet.

Good. Mia darts to the half bathroom quickly wiping her forehead and under her arms. She does a smell check, she's OK, for now but a shower needs to be in the very near future.

At the same time, Mike's car speeds down the street. As he turns into his driveway, the Dog Walking Woman is almost hit as she crosses in front of him. She hits the hood of his car. Mike yells, "Move bitch! Get out the way!" The dog walking woman scurries out of the way giving Mike the finger just as she'd given Mia earlier.

Mike aggressively pulls beside Mia's car but parks crooked. He jumps out of the car grabbing the cake, flowers, and gifts out as well. Then he sneaks toward the house like a burglar. Mike's cover is almost blown when the pretty neighbor yells good morning from across the street.

Mike turns around, sees the Pretty Neighbor jogging. She waves then blows him a kiss. He whispers loudly at her. "Shut. Da Fucq. Up! Don't you see I'm trying to sneak into my house." Oblivious to Mike's actions, the pretty neighbor says, "When are you going to show me the ceiling of your bedroom?"

Mike's head shoots toward the door seeing if Mia was anywhere around. He looks through the window but doesn't see her. He turns back to the pretty neighbor and waves her off like an annoying mosquito. Thinking Mike is being playful she finally says, "I'm free tomorrow! Byeeeee!!!" Then she jogs off.

For a brief second Mike regrets fucking someone so close to home, but that thought swiftly passes when he watches her ass bounce up and down as she jogs away. He snaps out of fantasizing about painting her ass again and returns to the mission at hand.

Mike makes it to the house. He looks through the window, sees nothing. Then goes to the door, covering the ring camera with his hand then puts his ear to the door. Listens. After a few beats, he slowly puts his hand on the doorknob. He turns it, slowly opening the door.

The front door creaks open, he winces at the sound. Then he hears Mia's voice calling from the kitchen.

"Baby is that you?"

Mike turns into the Waterboy as he stammers trying to get out a response.

"Uhh, yeah. Yeah babe it's me."

Mike hears a faint sizzling sound then he sniffs the hair smelling bacon and something sweet he can't put his finger on. Nevertheless, he takes a deep breath and rehearses what he's going to say when he sees Mia.

As he stands in the middle of the foyer, birthday gifts in hand, he wonders if it's going to be enough to curb her anger for missing her birthday yesterday. He's lost in his thoughts until Mia talks again.

"Good, you're just in time." Mike talks out loud to himself.

"Shit! Shit! Shit!" he thinks she's going to kill him.

Images of him walking into the kitchen and finding Mia there with an array of medieval weapons and Denise in a black hooded mask terrify his thoughts. He smells his shirt, then looks down at his clothes and notices his belt is undone. Dammit! He balances everything he's holding while trying to buckle it back. He calls back to Mia.

"OK, I'll be right there."

After he gets the belt situated, he steadies himself, then walks toward the kitchen.

Looking nervous, Mia sets out the last platter of food on the island. She's prepared a spread fit for a feast. She nervously looks around the kitchen, then at her clothes. She fixes her hair in her reflection in the microwave just as Mike enters with a carefree tone in his voice.

"Good morning my love. Happy birthday."

Startled, Mia turns around facing Mike. They both have a nervous look on their faces. Then Mia sees the gifts in Mike's hands. She walks over to him forcing a smile. On the way over to Mike, Mia thinks if she should react to the fact he's a day late and he spent the night out. Mike thinks if Mia will notice the same. But neither of them say anything about it. They pretend and exchange awkward pleasantries. Instead of giving Mike the smoke he deserves, Mia only says, "Aww thank you baby."

Mike gives Mia the gifts. She sits them in the chair then smells the flowers. She then opens the cake box looking down at a salon theme decorated cake with the words Happy Birthday mi amor. She fights back her emotions because Mike hasn't called her mi amor since freshman year in college. The phrase was the only one Mike cared to remember from their Spanish class where they first met.

She thinks it's sweet. It's the small things like this that makes it difficult for Mia to stay upset at Mike even though he deserves it. Every woman likes and appreciates the little things over some fake grand gesture anyway and Mia is no exception.

Mike stands behind her, lying.

"I got in pretty late last night and I didn't wanna wake you so I slept in the guest bedroom."

And just like that Mia's emotions turn back to anger. She knows without a doubt Mike is lying because if he actually slept in the guest bedroom he would have seen the mess she made of all the gifts.

However, on the other hand she's relieved at the lie because it means he doesn't know she spent the night out. Unfortunately for Mike, he just remembered he told Craig to say he slept at his house. What if Mia asks him later, he'd be caught in another lie. Instead of making it worse and trying to recover, he says nothing. Mia smirks and turns around to Mike with a little white lie of her own.

"That's OK. I was out cold. Denise threw me a party at the salon and I was beat."

It isn't completely a lie, not like Mike's, so she feels OK about it. They both awkwardly chuckle. Then at the same time, both breathe a sigh of relief. Mike looks at all the food and says, "I should be the one cooking. I'm the one who worked late and missed your birthday last night. I'm so sorry, I didn't even realize. I was so deep in paperwork and lost track of time."

Mia shrugs it off, seemingly unaffected, and says, "It's OK, sit down. Let's eat."

Mia puts the flowers down, grabs a plate and starts serving Mike. He looks a little relaxed but a little on edge at the same time. Mike looks at Mia with a peculiar look on his face. He inquires, "Sooo, uhhh, what did you get into last night?"

Mia drops the serving spoon at his question. The sound of the metal serving spoon makes Mike jump. *What's he implying? Does he suspect something?* She asks herself. An image of Terry kissing her back flashes in Mia's head. She lets out a soft ahhh then catches herself, swallowing hard, clears her throat before saying, "A bed. Umm the bed. Just the bed. I didn't work as hard as you."

Mia sets the plate down in front of Mike. She makes one for herself. Mike looks down at the food as an image of Nicole and Alisha kissing each other flashes in his head. He smiles, then catches himself.

"Yeah, it felt like I worked a double."

Mia turns around looking at Mike with a what the fuck face. She thinks to herself, *did this nigga just use code to say he had a threesome?* She knows damn well he wasn't working, he was with a bitch. Possibly two bitches. As Mia's thoughts run away, Mike stares at her like a deer in headlights. He asks himself, *damn did I say too much? Is she on to me?* He tells himself to keep calm. He puts food in his mouth and smiles as Mia stares at him.

Mia takes a seat. The cheating couple eat in silence, occasionally looking at each other when the other isn't looking. Both their phones chime at the same time.

They look up at each other with surprised looks on their faces unsure what to do. Mia picks up her phone first, then Mike. They both read their text messages. Mike's text message is from Nicole and Alisha thanking him for a great night and asking if he is free tomorrow. Mia gets a text from Terry asking if she's free next week.

She smacks her teeth. She explicitly told this fool not to text her and what does he do? Through the awkwardness, they both play it cool. Mike says it's a text about work. Mia says her text is from Denise.

They go back to eating their food. Mia looks at Mike thinking he has a lot of nerve to be eating the breakfast that she cooked acting like he didn't do anything. He waltzes up in the house with trinkets thinking everything is all good. It's her 40th birthday and all he has is flowers and a cake. He shoulda drove home a new car for her or something he doesn't normally get her when he fucks up.

As much as she wants to say something, she doesn't. The guilt is eating her up. Her one-time cheating seems like it holds so much weight over the countless times Mike has cheated. She tries so hard not to crack but finds strength in the fact that Mike's been cheating, especially last night.

Hating the silence, Mike looks up at Mia, he smiles and says tenderly.

"I love you."

Mia goes to say it back but she doesn't. She thinks to herself, *love shoulda brought your ass home last night*. Instead, she smiles and continues eating.

Later that day, Mia sings along to the SZA song playing from the overhead speakers. She has a pleasant look on her face. Mike stands in the doorway watching her. He can't believe she hasn't gone off on him yet. It's actually making him nervous, causing him to talk too much. Something that is unlike him. He asks, "Babe? You good?"

No I'm not good fool, she says to herself. She pushes that thought to the side and smiles at Mike saying, "Yeah baby. I'm fine."

Mike feels like she isn't fine. He thinks the bomb is about to drop any minute now. The uneasy feeling is killing him. It's like he rather her spazz out and get it over with. Something definitely feels off here but he can't put his finger on it.

"You just seem...different," he says. In between singing the SZA lyrics Mia says, "Maybe it's being 40 you know? It's having a positive effect on me. New year, new me I guess."

Mike continues to watch Mia now putting the folded clothes into the dresser drawers. He looks her up and down with a curious look on his face. This is new. This is scary.

But if she isn't going to say anything about last night, then he's not going to remind her. He merely nods his head saying OK. He looks at her one last time before leaving the room. Once he's gone, Mia sits on the bed looking toward the empty doorway. Mike's cavalier attitude is making keeping her secret easier than she thought. Strangely, she's grateful for it and has decided she will see Terry again.

A week later, Mike sits in the barber chair as the men in the shop erupt yelling NOOOOOO in unison. Proudly he nods his head yes.

"No cap." His barber shakes his head in disappointment.

"See that's how you young dudes get caught up. The number one rule when you cheat is.."

Everyone joins in saying, you always go home! Mike tries to defend himself.

"I know and I always did before but I ain't had two at a time since college. After the second time with both of them I was Pacquia'd, nodded. Out for the count."

Mike pretends to sleep, the barbershop laughs. One of the other barbers can't believe his ears and can't stop himself from asking, "Bruh, how are you still breathing? My lady woulda been killed me and smiled in her mugshot."

The men laugh again, Mike remains feeling successful with having gotten away with it.

"Man Mia didn't even notice. She was asleep before me as always."

One of the men proclaims Mike is lucky but Mike doesn't see it that way. He takes the win as a testament of how good he is. Unbeknownst to the men though, there is one thing that bothers him. The fact that Mia cooked. She hasn't cooked for him in months and she cooked for *him* after he missed *her* birthday.

Mike stands outside the barbershop texting on his phone. Allison, a black, 40's year old stunning woman, carrying shopping bags walks toward Mike. She sees him, removes her sunglasses as she checks him out. She likes what she sees and decides to shoot her shot.

"I love a man with a fresh cut."

Mike looks up from his phone, makes eye contact with Allison, smiles.

"Well, let me help you get a better view." Mike playfully poses allowing Allison to get a good look.

Allison walks around Mike looking at him from head to toe and taking a long hard look at his groin.

"Trust me baby, I am."

She introduces herself to him. Mike shakes her hand, noticing the wedding ring. He makes eye contact with Allison raising an eyebrow at the ring. He should walk away but he doesn't, his confidence has been kicked up a few notches from the men in the barbershop so he begins to flirt.

"You think that's gonna deter me from shooting my shot?" he asks. Allison giggles, Mike doesn't get what's so funny. She says, "I'm the one shooting my shot here, not you. But it's cute you think so."

Mike chuckles as she kisses the back of Allison's hand then asks if she's hungry. She lets out a bored sigh then talks matter of factly.

"Let's cut to the chase. You want sex."

Mike is taken aback by Allison's forwardness. Women come at him on a daily basis, he doesn't have to put in much effort but there's something different about Allison. He's intrigued.

At that moment, Mike doesn't know what to say and it shows all over his face. Allison helps him out.

"It's cool cause I want sex. But I like a different kinda sex."

Mike raises an eyebrow. This just got very interesting. He checks Allison out for the first time and is impressed. For her age she has the body of the two women he just spent the night with. But is she as freaky as them? *Wait, maybe she's nasty*, he thinks to himself. And he's all too eager to learn if he's right. He asks Allison, "How different?"

Allison doesn't respond, she just licks her lips staring at Mike seductively. She then looks toward the parking lot then to Mike asking, "Which car is yours?"

Mike points to the black Mercedes AMG parked next to a Porsche SUV.

"Good, follow me."

Before Mike could say a word Allison walked away headed toward the Porsche. Mike smiles, chuckling to himself. He likes that Allison is seemingly on his level financially which is one of the criteria for deciding if he's going to have sex with a woman or not. Plus she's married, she has just as much to lose as he does. The playing field is even, making Mike's decision, if there ever was a doubt, to follow Allison. The two end up in the same hotel Terry had taken Mia to but the different type of sex Allison mentioned was something that Mike would have never thought about. Allison is dressed up in a Power Rangers costume. She stands in front of Mike holding a costume out for him.

Mike doesn't know what to do. The only thought in his mind is, this is some white people comic-con type of shit. His mind and feet say run Forrest run! But his dick says, relax, this could be fun. Mike ultimately decides to decline. "Oh hell naww!! What kinda cosplay freaky deeky ish you into?"

Allison groans in frustration. She takes a deep breath trying not to get upset. She explains.

"I can have regular sex with my husband. If I'm going to have an affair then it's gonna be something my husband won't do. This is it. Don't you have any wild fantasies you want to live out?" Mike thinks.

"Yeah but they include less clothes, a yacht and Beyonce."

Allison shows a sign of immaturity by stomping her feet like a spoiled child.

"Com'on, you scared of a little role play?" Mike starts laughing.

He can't see Allison's face through her helmet but she's not amused, she's deadass serious.

"I'm just not sure if you wanna fight me or fuck me."

Allison walks to Mike pressing her titis against his chest. She says, "Then put the costume on and find out."

Mike thinks. Allison steps back, handing him the suit again. Reluctantly Mike takes it, examining it. He asks, "Do I really have to put the helmet on?"

Meanwhile, at the salon, Mia is telling Denise a story of her own but Denise has her face turned up.

"I don't wanna hear about you cooking for Mike. Tell me about Terrrryyyy. How big was it again?"

Mia sticks her tongue out like Cardi B remembering Terry's length, girth and stamina. She squeezes her legs closed at the thought of it. She looks at Denise.

"You ever seen a Louisville slugger?"

Denise closes her eyes, slides down to the floor enjoying the thought. The other women in the salon hoot and holler, high-fiving each other. Mia giggles like a smitten schoolgirl. Denise yells out, "Biiiitch!!"

Mia tries to play it off.

"I mean I wasn't that impressed. Mike packs like that." The women in the salon booo at the mention of Mike. As Denise finally gets off the floor, she protests, "Who cares about Mike!?"

The women all agree. Mia looks at them confused, almost insulted.

"Damn, OK."

A stylist chimes in congratulating Mia for getting some good Jeremiah for her birthday. Mia looks confused again missing the reference. The women see the blank look on her face and join in singing BIRTHDAY SEX! BIRTHDAY SEX! They sing and dance for a few minutes, Mia sits back watching and laughing thinking the women are a mess but the reassurance is exactly what she needs.

Denise then addresses the question that's on every woman's mind, they want to know when she's going to see Terry again. Everyone stops what they're doing, looks at Mia. She avoids eye contact with everyone. She's already accepted Terry's invitation to hook up with him and today is the day but she's not about to tell them that. She's already shared enough and has a small fear that it could get back to Mike.

She looks at everyone and lies.

"It was a one-time thing."

The women look at Mia as if they don't believe her. Denise has a very unpleasant look on her face. Mia looks at the women's faces of disappointment. She sighs, smiles.

"I may or may not have a lunch date with him today."

The shop erupts with a loud YAAAAASSSSS! The women cheer, clap and snap with excitement, Mia laughs shaking her head.

Later, Terry sits in the same hotel lobby as before. He anxiously taps a room key on his leg as he doesn't take his eyes off the sliding doors.

Mia hands her keys to the valet wearing a long dark coat, black hat and sunglasses. She doesn't say anything to him as she scurries into the hotel lobby. Inside, she cautiously looks around her heart beating a mile a minute.

She can't understand why she's so nervous, it's not like Mike found out about the first time, so what's the issue?

Maybe she thinks it's a little different this time. Last week was supposed to be a one-time thing. A small part of her wanted to go out and find someone to have meaningless sex with then never see them again. But this time it's a little more intentional. She thought last week was the shock to her system she needed to get over being stood up by Mike but she can't stop thinking about Terry.

Then again, maybe it's not Terry but just the idea of doing it and not feeling guilty about it. Guilt aside, she still doesn't want to get caught, people know her and those same people know Mike. So if her nerves help her be more cautious, then dressing like a private detective and acting like she's dodging paparazzi is what has to happen.

Inside the lobby she frantically searches for Terry but is too jittery to see he's sitting a few feet in front of her across the lobby. Finally she spots him then hurries over.

She stands in front of him. She reaches him, Terry smiles standing up and going in for a hug.

"There she is."

The two hug, Terry finishes with a kiss on the cheek but Mia pushes him away.

"No, not in public."

Mia pulls her hat down as she looks around. Terry laughs, ensuring Mia that no one is gonna notice her. "You're a ball player, and camera phones are everywhere. Next thing you know I'm on the Shade Room labeled the side chick." Terry laughs again.

Mia pulls down her sunglasses giving Terry a serious look.

"Is that why you're dressed like the pink panther?"

Mia playfully hits Terry in his arm allowing herself to join in the laugh despite it being at her expense.

"Whatever. Just leave a key at the counter next time."

"Yeah but you need to show your ID to get the key," Terry reminds her.

Mia thinks. Damn he's right.

"Well, well, then just tell me the room number and meet me there. Now com'on, we've been standing here too long."

Mia grabs Terry by the arm struggling to drag him with her to the elevator.

Two hours later, Mia and Terry lay on their back glistening with sweat and pleased smiles on their faces. Terry turns on his side looking at Mia, she turns to him. She wants to ask him a question and it's eating at her. She wants to ask because that's the type of person she is but she doesn't want to overstep and seem like she's insecure about the unsaid arrangement.

She and Terry have not discussed what happens after today. A part of her wants to make this a regular thing but she's unsure if that is what he wants. She starts to second guess the reason she's even here. Terry must have a gang of women he's either dealing with or can choose from. His wife must be gorgeous, ball players marry the prom queen not the captain of the chess team. Mia wonders what she's like. Is she prettier than her? What's she not doing for Terry that he feels like he's getting from Mia.

With so many thoughts running through Mia's mind, she's gotten from her original thought. She then figures she has nothing to lose. If the question upsets Terry and he never wants to see her again then that's her way out and this wasn't supposed to be an ongoing thing.

"How many women have you cheated on your wife with?" Terry chuckles without hesitation.

The question didn't catch him off guard and he has nothing to hide but he tells her that it doesn't matter. Mia sits up covering herself with the sheet. She looks down at Terry looking at her with a boyish grin. She scoffs, "It does if we're not using protection." Terry nods. He understands Mia's concern, it's valid.

"Then the question should be if I'm sleeping with anyone else." He gets quiet. Mia's face demands an answer. "OK, are you?"

"Other than you and my wife, no."

Mia smacks her teeth in disbelief as she flops back onto the bed. She thinks to herself, niggas be lyin'.

She looks Terry in the eyes and she sees truth in them. Honesty in his voice. Her defenses come down, she believes him. She doesn't want to, it would be easier to think he's a lying ass man and walk away. But she doesn't want to. She's afraid, this all has happened too easy. Too quickly. It would be foolish of her to take his word, she needs more proof.

Mia holds her hand out and demands Terry's phone from him. To her surprise, Terry doesn't put up a fight. He rolls over to the nightstand retrieving it and handing it to her. Mia can't believe it. Just like that he gave it to her. Mike would never willingly give her his phone. She's never asked but she knows how Mike is. Terry is proving himself to be different. She melts a little bit but she channels her inner Denise and goes through the phone anyway.

She first scrolls through his text messages and asks about every female name she sees. It feels like Terry answers honestly stating which name is his wife, which one is his mother and sister and one being his manager. Mia should feel satisfied but she isn't, he continues her deep dive into Terry's phone as he puts his hands behind his head looking relaxed.

Mia then goes to Terry's photo album, scrolls, only finding pictures of Terry on the court or at events.

This peaks her interest. She looks at Terry calling him a narcissist for only having pictures of himself on his phone. "What's wrong with that?" Mia continues looking. "There isn't one picture of your wife in here."

Terry doesn't see that as a problem but Mia finds it very strange. Is Terry even married? But why would he lie about it if he wasn't. That would be a strange way to pick up women to lie about being married. Mia would think that would be a deterrent.

Next she checks his Instagram feed. To her surprise there are no posts of big booty women twerking and no one has slid in his DM's. Mia doesn't know what to say.

Unable to find any evidence that Terry isn't running around slangin' dick to multiple women, Mia exits and hands Terry back his phone.

"I gotta go."

She says not wanting to overstay at the hotel. After all, she does have two hair salons to run. Mia and Terry get out of the bed and put their clothes on in silence, occasionally exchanging flirtatious glances at each other. Worried someone would see them together, Mia says, "Let me go out first. I'll text you when I'm in the car." Terry obliges and watches Mia leave the room.

Mia exits the hotel room resting her back on the door. A smile comes on her face. She's smitten and she knows it. It's not about the sex, even though it's really, really good sex. But she loves Terry's unwavering transparency. It's a form of honesty that she's never experienced from Mike. It's refreshing and more than enough for her to continue seeing him, for as long as he wants to see her.

For Mia, honesty holds more weight than all the lavish and expensive gifts in the world. It's really the only thing she's ever wanted from Mike, that and monogamy. She walks toward the elevator sorting out all the thoughts in her mind. This is a new feeling for her and it isn't going unnoticed.

Her love for Mike is still there and she doesn't think that will ever change. What she has going on with Terry is only adding to the relationship. He's giving her the one thing that's missing which is the honesty. In the midst of her thoughts, Mia made sure to reassure herself that despite the way Terry makes her feel, she won't fall in love.

She's already cheating on her husband but falling in love will open up a whole different issue. If she falls in love with Terry she's going to have a decision to make. And that decision will never work out in her favor. Why? Because Terry isn't sleeping with her because he's upset with his wife. They have an understanding. Both of them know what it is and they are acting accordingly.

Just three floors above where Terry and Mia made headboard music, Mike and Allison lay in the bed next to each other covered in the sheets but still have on the Power Rangers helmets trying to catch their breath.

Mike is blown away. He has no idea what just happened but he loves it and can't stop thinking about it. He looks over at Allison, her perky C-cup breasts rising up and down with every breath and her 4-pack ab stomach is a vision. As weird as it may seem, looking at her semi exposed naked body and wearing the pink ranger helmet is a turn on and he's ready to go again.

The couple lay in silence until Mike finally breaks it, "No cap, I don't know what we just did but I wanna do it again."

Allison laughs taking off her helmet, Mike follows suit. He takes a deep breath taking in a lot of air as if he's been holding his breath underwater for an extended amount of time.

"I told you you'd like it."

Mike nods his head smiling big.

"It's like I was in my body but kinda not, like damn!" Allison explains to Mike why it was so good. She says that's what happens when you let go and live in the moment. She continues by stating sex should be an experimental experience. It's not all about gettin' a nut, that's the bonus part. The exploration makes for a better orgasm.

Mike agrees, it's something he's never thought about in that level of depth before. Not only is Allison extremely sexy and kinky but she has a brain, she thinks about things which adds to Mike's attraction to her.

Allison sits up looking at Mike. Her face is very stern and serious as she speaks.

"I shoulda said this before we started but if we're gonna do this again, I have to set a few ground rules." Mike turns to her with his full attention.

Allison makes it known off the bat that this isn't meant to be a one-time thing. It is her desire, but sounds more like a demand, to see Mike twice a week. Same time. Same room. Her rules continue with no phone calls or meetups after 5 p.m. which works for Mike because he won't have to worry about spending the night out again. He agrees and allows Allison to continue.

Allison goes on to instruct Mike to erase his text messages everyday before going home. She warns him, "'Cause if your wife calls me I'ma send her a pic of my ass with Mike was here written on it."

Mike bursts out laughing but Allison ensures him that she's deadass. She lets Mike finish getting the laugh out of his system.

"I hear you. Is that all?"

Allison sits up looking more serious than when she started. She leans in close to Mike's face pointing her finger at him.

"Absolutely no gifts. Ever."

Mike answers done without any hesitation. All of Allisons requirements are more than easy for Mike to adhere to. He doesn't outwardly express his joy for not having to wine and dine a woman of Allison's stature.

By looking at her one would think that she's very high maintenance. Her husband obviously is a man of means, he would have to be to keep up with a woman like Allison if she made her own money. She spares no expense on her appearance. Judging by his knowledge of hair after spending countless hours with Mia looking at different units when she was opening her first salon, Mike could tell that Allison's hair is nearly a thousand dollars.

Her beat face is flawless assuming it's from Rhianna's Savage Fenty collection because her bra and panties are the same brand, from the high-end line. Diamond earrings, diamond platinum Cuban link necklace, a diamond and rose gold bracelet and a rare Patek Phillipe watch all of which she kept on during sex convinces Mike he's right in his assumptions on her wealth. But it doesn't matter, she doesn't want gifts, Mike's wallet is safe. All she wants is the D on her terms and why would Mike not oblige?

Mike has never said it out loud but it does get tiring meeting someone new, knocking them down then doing the process all over again. He used to think having so many women out there it's only a matter of time until one of them gets upset for whatever reason and shows up at his house. That's his biggest fear. No not getting caught but Mia actually having to come face to face with his indiscretions like she did before they were married.

He can remember the look on her face, it was the first time he truly felt remorse for going outside of their relationship and he never wants to feel that feeling again or put Mia through that. It's for that reason why Allison's agreement works out. Her sexual intelligence far exceeds anyone he's been with in the past. And even though he's never thought about it before, he is enthusiastic with the idea of role playing and finding out just how deep Allison's kink goes. He hopes Allison is into group play or at least other women. That would be the icing on the cake.

Mike returns his attention back to Allison as she lays back on the bed. He gets on top of her, she opens her legs making it easier and the two kiss passionately. Afterwards, Mike smirks as he raises his hips looking at her fresh wax then looks at her.

"Now that these helmets aren't in the way, how about some FaceTime?" Allison giggles and replies, "What you waiting for?" She pushes Mike's head down between her legs.

122

Chapter 5

Back at home and in a great mood having just had multiple orgasms, Mia puts food into a Tupperware container. Beside her sits a post-it note and a red sharpie. She writes "enjoy my love" on the note before sticking it on top then puts it in the microwave. She wipes off the counter, turns off the light then leaves the kitchen.

She looks around at the clean chef's kitchen with a smile before turning off the light and leaving. She heads for the stairs when she hears Mike coming through the front door. She turns around to him with a loving smile. Mike sees her upon entering, he smiles and says hey.

Mia runs into Mike's arms throwing her arms around his neck to his surprise and kisses him deeply. Mike doesn't know what to do. It's been longer than he can care to remember but he's not going to fight it. He wraps his arms around her and the two kiss as if he'd just returned home from war. They both enjoy the kiss feeling as if they'd reconnected with each other. From Mia's standpoint it is because of Mike that she's this happy. If it weren't for missing her birthday she wouldn't have found what she's been missing. For Mike it feels good to have Mia close to him.

After they finish kissing, Mia keeps her arms wrapped around Mike's neck. She looks at his lips and glistening beard. Mike becomes worried she can taste Allison, but remembers he washed his beard with the cheap hotel soap before leaving.

Mia wipes her lipstick off Mike's bottom lip and looks him in the eye.

"I put your dinner in the microwave. I'm going to bed. Goodnight."

She kisses him one last time before heading upstairs. Mike stands there dumbfounded, mouth agape and his eyes fixed on Mia's ass while she walks upstairs looking back at him smiling. Finally his mind starts working again and he says, "Uuhhh thanks. Goodnight. I love you."

At the top of the stairs Mia returns the I love you then turns the corner out of sight. Still stuck like Chuck, Mike asks himself where did this sudden change come from? Maybe she got tired of being petty with him. But why? What's changed?

In the middle of Mike trying to figure out why Mia is acting so different after so long, his stomach grumbles. He enters the kitchen cautiously opening the microwave. Mike retrieves the Tupperware looking down at the note. He reads it to himself trying to be happy but is still suspicious.

He removes the lid looking inside to find the meal Mia made the very first time she cooked for him.

Orange and ginger salmon with brown rice and as-paragus. Mike leans in, smells it to ensure Mia didn't do something to the food. This could just be another one of her petty moments. She could have cooked for him and doused the food with an extreme amount of salt. He notices the food is still warm.

He suspiciously licks the top of the salmon. It's good! Just the right amount of salt and other seasonings. Re-membering the scene from the movie Why Did I Get Married when Tasha cooked for her husband after a spat of fighting, Mike has it in his mind that some-thing is up. But he remembers what the character said.

She realized she was being hard on her husband and wanted to show her appreciation for everything he's done and to say she's sorry. Maybe this is the same situation. *Damn, maybe art does imitate life*, he thinks to himself. He shakes off the thoughts of Mia having an ulterior motive for cooking for him and grabs a fork sitting down at the island to eat. He takes the first bite. His eyes roll in the back of his head as he savors the food.

Upstairs, Mia enters the room and flops on the edge of the bed with her purse. She removes a wrapped gift box. She stares at it. On her way home she stopped at the mall to pick up a little something for Mike. She purchased a black and white gold Audemars Piguet watch.

A few weeks ago Mike had left a page up on his iPad browser of the watch but he never bought it, so she bought it for him. She contemplates going down-stairs to give it to him. Then she thinks about leaving it on his pillow to find when he comes to bed. But she doesn't do either.

A gift like this, out of the blue, would certainly raise some suspicion from Mike. But it was only fitting that she followed Mike's lead and buy a gift because she had sex with someone else. Mia knows all men are dumb but she's not too naive to think Mike wouldn't put two and two together.

She exhales, looking around the room for the right place to hide it hoping that if Mike stumbled on it he would think it's for his birthday which is coming up in four months. She can't hide it in the room though, so where? Maybe in the guest closet with all her gifts but that means she'd have to clean up the mess she made when she shoved everything back in last week. She rejects that idea.

Where is the one place that a man would think to look last? Mia leaps to her feet and sneaks into the hallway. She stops, listens. She can hear Mike's fork scraping against the Tupperware and his light smacking. With the coast clear, she heads to the linen closet.

Mia decides to put the watch box behind a set of sheets on the top shelf but struggles to reach it. She then puts it behind the towels on the middle shelf. Yeah, he'll never come in here. Mia closes the door satisfied with her hiding place then returns back to the bedroom.

Over the next several weeks Mike and Mia continue to have their extramarital affairs without either of them finding out. After the second time with

Terry, all of Mia's reservations have gone out of the window. Denise's advice to just go with it definitely played a part in the process.

There's something about doing a thing you know you shouldn't be doing especially if it has devastating consequences that adds to the allure of it. Mia's never cheated in her life. She saw how much her father's infidelity affected her mother, ultimately leading them to divorce right as she left for college.

Mia rationalized her actions with the idea that even if Mike did find out, he's in no position to be upset enough to break up the marriage. And if he does, there's no prenup so that's that.

The only thing that really would be hurt is Mike's ego. He wouldn't dare tell Clive or any of his buddies at work and he most certainly won't walk into the barbershop and let the men there know she gave him a taste of his own medicine.

Mia's not the type of woman to openly or purposely embarrass Mike. She understands how fragile a man's ego and reputation is. No matter how much in the wrong he is, she wouldn't do that to him. So if he did find out about her and Terry, she wouldn't say a word. Their shared silence benefits them both.

Unfortunately, Mia thinks the problem is Mike freely runs around doing the same thing expecting karma not to catch up with him. That's where he messed up, thinking she would continue to be so docile that she wouldn't do it too. The singer Sparkle once said, when a woman's fed up, there ain't nothing you can do about it.

With that said, Mia continues with seeing Terry once a week, sometimes two and three times and

Mike is none the wiser. He is still happy with Mia, dinner and sex on the regular. Mia and Terry's sex is more like a friends with benefits situation, with a big enthusiasm on the friends part.

Sometimes they don't have sex. They do little things like play cards and laugh. Mia and Terry are both big foodies so Grubhub and UberEats have become their best friends since they can't be seen in public. They've expanded each other's tastes and pallets in cuisine and it's extended to movies. For Mia, the best thing, outside of the sex is when they just lay with each other talking. Real intimacy.

Terry expressed how his wife is always on the go managing her real estate empire and that she doesn't take opportunities to spend quality time with Terry. That's why they have an arrangement. He and his wife schedule sex around what she has going on. There are no dinner nights at home, no time spending watching trash TV. If she isn't showing a house, dealing with issues that arise with the properties or negotiating a contract, she's on the phone. The only real time Terry spends with his wife is when the two have to show up at an event, whether it's for him or for her. Talking to Mia, Terry understood that he may have made his wife this way. When he was a professional basketball player his wife was always left alone when he was on the road or in practice. She had to find something to occupy her time being that she's not a "real housewife" type of woman.

During his career she built her empire, now worth millions but unfortunately for Terry, she didn't retire when he did. It's not like the couple needs the money. Terry was very smart with the money and endorsements he's made during his career. But his wife has made her own money and she loves the freedom. He thinks now it's a part of her identity which is making it hard for her to take a step back.

Nevertheless, Terry still very much loves his wife. After all it takes a special type of woman to knowingly allow her husband to sleep with other women. Mia was super impressed by the fact that Terry told her he was completely faithful while he was in the NBA when a lot of men weren't. The arrangement Terry now has with his wife is a new thing, it's only been in place the last four years since his retirement from the league.

On this particular day, while watching Tyler Perry's Why Did I get Married, Mia and Terry spoke about the 80/20 rule. He explained that while the rule may work for some people, that rule didn't work for him. He said he was always taught to do everything one hundred percent as well as not accepting anything less from people in his life.

Therefore he couldn't be completely happy without the twenty percent that was missing in his marriage. During that conversation, Mia realized that she once was happy with the 80 percent that Mike was giving her. She hadn't realized how much of the impact the other 20 percent had once she realized it was missing. She thought about the concept and a question about Terry and his marriage began burning in her mind. So she decided to come out with it and ask.

"I guess I wanna ask you because I'm afraid to ask my husband but, instead of having an affair, why don't you just leave your wife?"

Terry chuckles at the questions, he knew eventually she would bring it up. He's prepared with an answer, the truth not a lie. Terry looks at Mia as she anxiously awaits an answer.

"That's easy. Because I love her."

Mia scoffs at that answer. What type of answer is that anyway. Mia thinks that if he really loved her he would be doing the opposite. She can't fathom that being the actual answer, so she presses him to elaborate.

"How much can you really love her if you cheat on her? Like how do men justify that?"

Terry nods his head and asks Mia how many friends she have? She's taken aback by the question thinking Terry is avoiding the question at hand. She asks him why is that important? But Terry won't answer her question until she answers his adding that it'll better help him answer hers. Mia takes a beat, wanting the answer but feeling like Terry is playing games. Remembering he's always kept it one hundred with her, she concedes and answers.

"OK, I have three really good friends." Terry says, "Right. And each of those people are different and they serve a different purpose, right?"

Mia nods in agreement, Terry continues. He explains that cheating is almost like having multiple friends, taking it back to the 80/20 rule. He states that a person knows which friend can keep a secret. Which friend would help you hide a body without asking any questions or which friend will tell you what you want to hear but more importantly what you need to hear.

Mia listens with her full attention while Terry continues to talk. He goes on by saying when a man cheats, it's because he's getting something from another woman that his main chick isn't giving or willing to give. But just like you don't stop talking to one friend because they don't do what the other friend does, you keep them all. The same is true in a relationship. I can get what I need from you and go home and still love my wife for the things she provides. Essentially, you don't throw the baby away with the bath water.

Mia thinks. Terry makes sense, but he also doesn't make sense. Maybe it's the way the female brain is wired that's preventing her from completely understanding the concept. As she thinks, her inquisitive face turns sad, Terry notices.

"Are you bothered by my explanation?" Mia doesn't answer, she falls deep into her inner thoughts as if someone tapped the side of a teacup. She thought back on the pettiness she had displayed in the first six years of her marriage and understood it was a result of the missing 20 percent. With more thought, she came to the conclusion that it was less about Mike cheating and him spending time with other women. Time he should have been spending with her. Now, she's still not cool with Mike sleeping with other women but she questions if Mike is missing something like she was.

Was she not giving him the amount of sex that he required? Was she not experimental enough in the bedroom? Was the toppy not sloppy enough? Was the buckshot not shooting? These are all questions she's never stopped to ask Mike. Seriously, how many women or men actually talk to their partner about their sex life and performance? Maybe this whole thing could have been avoided if she'd just asked. She can't expect a man to come out and say it, they're not built that way.

Doing the introspective work on her own potential shortcomings, Mia also realized that you don't know what you don't know. If she hadn't met Terry, she may still be unhappy in an 80 percent marriage. There is one thing that Mia has noticed since she's started sleeping with Terry, Mike has stopped buying gifts. She questions what this could mean. Has he stopped cheating? If he has stopped cheating, should she break things off with Terry? She immediately shook that thought off. Like Terry explained, some people need 100 percent and not just the 80.

Unlike Mia, Mike isn't having any of those thoughts. He is too busy taking full advantage of getting 100 percent from Allison. Each time they meet, Allison has a new costume and role-playing activity for them. One day they dressed as Simpson characters inspired by Cardi B's 2022 Halloween costume. Another day they're breaking the rules by having sex in the hotel pool dressed as the Joker and Harley Quinn. Their sinister laughter and moaning scared people from coming into the pool so much so that the manager had to intervene.

Understandably uncomfortable, the hotel manager tried his best not to look at Mike and Allison naked. He shook his head while looking at their red and blue body paint smeared on the diving board as he asked them to go back to their room. After climaxing, Mike and Allison walked proudly out of the pool without any clothes on.

Allison refused a towel from the hotel manager. She struts past a visiting family with three small children giving them an eyeful of the smeared body paint exposing her most intimate parts. One 11-year-old boy got smacked upside his head when he stared at Allison's butt.

Unlike Mia and Terry, Mike and Allison don't do pillow talk, movies or eat food. They have wild, sweaty, comic-con type sex then they say their good-byes. They don't share anything personal about themselves but they don't need to.

Allison believes that she can learn all she needs to know about a man from sex. But it's not like Mike is looking for a "friend" anyway. The sex with Allison is so mind-blowing that he doesn't want or need anything else. If he could change one thing about his encounters with Allison is the timer she puts on her phone signaling it's time for her to head back out. He understands a woman running a business, Mia runs two salons. However, she still makes time to cook and chill.

It took speaking to Dr. Phil for Mike to realize that he's in two "non- monogamous" relationships. He's committed by law to Mia of course, but he's only sleeping with Allison. No it isn't a requirement for Allison, she could care less if Mike is seeing other women, it's actually a choice he's made on his own.

Mike is satisfied, it's as simple as that. Mia has stopped with her foolishness around the house and they're in a good space. His stomach is full and his balls stay empty. Mia is none the wiser and his credit card is getting some relief because he's not buying gifts after each new woman he cheats with. What more can a man want? Mike is no exception.

On his drives home from work, Mike often thinks about revealing his relationship with Allison to Mia. He hasn't caught feelings for Allison but like Mia, he doesn't want to cut things off with her. He thinks it's just a matter of time before one of them does. The devil on his shoulder doesn't want him to though. Like why mess up a good thing? He's happy, Mia's seemingly happy so why introduce a problem when you don't have to?

For the first time ever, Mike feels some kind of regret. He understands he's been cheating their entire relationship but as of late, it's felt different. He feels a little guilt and he doesn't know where it's coming from. Mike doesn't like the feeling and tries his best to shake it off before he pulls in the driveway and has to face Mia. As he parks the car looking at his wedding band, he turns his attention to the house. He looks at it feeling an immense warm feeling inside. Mike sikes himself up not to say anything.

He's going to put on his brave Mike face and act like everything is all good. At least until he can talk to the fellas at the barbershop for a little advice. Maybe Dr. Phil can offer up something but what does he know? He's been with the same woman forever, he ain't out here in these streets gettin' it like Mike, so what can he tell him?

Mike enters the house to the sweet smell of vanilla candles. Mia calls from the dining room.

"Take your shoes off please."

Mike looks confused, as the request is a new one but he obliges her then walks into the dining room.

The dining room table is set for a romantic candle lit dinner. Mia's brought out the good china they've gotten as a wedding present along with the gold spoons that Clive gifted them. Mia walks from the kitchen to the dining room setting down enough dishes with different ingredients to rival chipotle. Mike looks at the table with gratitude for not only the food but the effort Mia has gone through.

The pico looks and smells fresh, hand prepared. Mia has an assortment of hard and soft tacos, sour cream, and real Mexican cheese, cotija. Lastly, the slow cooker sits in the middle of a ring of tortilla chips. Mia enters the room snapping Mike out of his food trance.

"I know it's not Tuesday, but I was craving tacos and I didn't wanna order any fast food so..."

Mia sets down the large serving bowl of season steaming chicken. She smiles at Mike, he smiles back then walks over to him throwing her arms around him.

"I've missed you," she whispers in his ear.

Mike hugs her tighter, closing his eyes savoring the smell of her perfume. The couple fall into a deep intimate hug while Mike feels stronger guilt in the pit of his stomach. Mia kisses him on the cheek before letting go.

"I didn't know what you wanted but I didn't wanna spoil the surprise by calling."

Mike looks down at the food one more time, then back at Mia. He smiles not wanting to tell her that despite the thoughtfulness of her, he would have preferred beef instead of chicken.

He thinks being honest at this point would most certainly ruin the moment so he pushes it back. The smile and proud look on Mia's face is more than enough for him to eat the chicken. He's not going to take this moment from her.

"Chicken is cool, all this looks great!" Mia reads Mike's face, she smirks talking playfully as she mocks him. "Chicken is cool."

Mia and Mike break out into a laugh, a real genuine one. To them both, this feels like their college days when they laughed about any and everything each other did.

"What?! It is, for real."

Mia looks Mike up and down with a devious look in her eye.

"I'll be right back."

Mia quickly walks into the kitchen. Mike takes a seat at the table thinking what could she be bringing back now? What, or more terrifying, who could be in the kitchen? Is the neighbor that's been blowing up his phone these past few weeks? Could it be the chef he fired once Mia started cooking again?

Mike's heart begins to beat out of his chest. He trembles, taps his leg nervously. All of the bad vibes Mike is feeling went away when Mia came back into the dining room smiling and holding a serving plate of barrio tacos. Mike's face lights up. He laughs and claps. Mia is pleased at his response knowing what he really wanted.

"You know I know you, right?"

Mike nods his head smiling.

"Yes, you do."

Mia sets the plate down in front of him.

"These are for you, the chicken is for me. I'm watching my beef intake."

Mike comedically looks at Mia as if she's lost her mind. "You better start that tomorrow, cause you gettin' this beef tonight!" Mia laughs loudly, Mike joins in.

Finally Mia takes a seat beside him, not on the other end of the table like usual. Mike looks at Mia lovingly, she holds out her hand, he takes it. Squeezes.

"I love you," says Mike.

"I love you too baby," Mia responds.

Later that night Mia and Mike didn't have sex. They made love. They both were very intentional with every touch, stroke and thrust. Mike's gentle warm tongue glided down Mia's stomach then made circles around her navel before making its way to her freshly steamed yoni. Her hips raised with each lick allowing Mike to grip her ass more firmly and stop her from running away when the pleasure got to be too much.

Mike took his time and enjoyed his wife being deliberate with everything he did. He remembered how she likes to be bent slightly over the edge of the bed because it gives her the perfect arch. He called her the names that brings the inner freak out of her a little more. Mia flinches just a little when Mike applies the right amount of pressure when he's biting her neck.

Mike didn't think about Allison during sex with Mia and Mia didn't think about Terry. They were completely consumed with each other, like a married couple should be. It's the type of sex they haven't had as a married couple. It's almost as if Mike and Mia were able to be free and be in the moment. One would think, would they have been able to do that if they weren't exploring other things with outside people?

After finishing for the third time, Mike and Mia's bed had no sheets, pillows or blankets left, they were all scattered around the room. They lay next to each other in multiple wet spots but not giving a care in the world about it. They both are panting heavily, Mia's hair wild and out of control.

The sweat glistening on her bare breast looks like the moonlight dancing on the ocean on a clear night.

Mike's face is covered with sweat and the remembrance of Mia's nectar juices which he can still smell in his beard, he smiles at the scent of it. The two look over at each other giggling and staring into their eyes trying to find the right word to express how they feel. Happy. That's the simplest and purest word to use.

Mia looks at Mike, the man she fell in love with freshman year, despite the beard he still looks the same. She remembers how she felt in that moment because she feels that way now. Mike looks at her remembering why he approached her that fateful day in the courtyard. He wasn't the type to approach women due to them always throwing themselves at him.

There was something about her that day. Before she even said a word or flashed a smile, he knew that she would be the woman he'd marry, eventually no matter how hard he tried to fight against it. And fight he did.

Mia rolls over on her side, resting her head on the palm of her hand, smiling.

"Thank you."

Mike looks confused. His face asks what is she thanking him for? Mia sees and responds.

"It's one thing to know you love me, but to feel it and experience it like we just did. It means more. It feels different. Feels better."

Not one for words, Mike just smiles and nods his head. Mia made him feel all warm and fuzzy on the inside.

He rolls over giving Mia a soft kiss on the lips. She giggles at the tickle of his beard. Mike says, "How about we both skip work tomorrow and spend the day together?" Mia's eyes light up.

"Really? You mean that?" Mike laughs.

"Yes. Anything you wanna do, we'll do." Mia thinks, "Ohh, I wanna have brunch at Toast on Lenox in midtown."

Mike nods yes, Mia continues.

"Then I wanna go play golf. Like real golf, not top golf." Mike's surprised.

"Golf? Since when do you like playing golf?"

Mia shrugs her shoulders.

"I don't know. I guess I wanna try something new." "OK, cool, I'm game. Anything else?" Mia thinks again then lays on Mike's chest.

"I don't know. Let's just see where the day and night take us."

Chapter 6

Mia holds onto Mike's hand tightly as the two cruise out of their neighborhood with the top down. At the stop sign Mike sees the sexy neighbor jogging toward them. He tenses up and avoids eye contact hoping she doesn't make a scene. When she sees him she smiles and waves. "Hi Mia!" Mia looks across Mike and waves back at the sexy neighbor. Mike is confused yet relieved.

They continue driving but Mike can't help but to ask. "Who was that?" Mia bobs to the music as she answers. "That's Michelle. She lives on our block. I did her hair a few weeks ago. Nice woman. She said she sees you out running sometimes." "Oh is that all she said?" Mike asks hoping there was nothing more to their conversation. "About you? Yeah."

Mike nods. "Oh speaking of which, I gotta stop by the salon real quick." Mike's head shoots in Mia's direction looking disappointed.

"We said we were skipping work today."

Mia grabs Mike's arm tightly leaning over resting her head on his shoulder in efforts to make him feel better.

"I know baby but I just gotta check on one thing and I promise I'll be yours for the rest of the day."

Grudgingly, Mike agrees.

The car stops in front of Mia's salon. As she takes off her seat belt she looks over at Mike who isn't moving.

"You're not coming in with me?" Mike shakes his head no. Mia playfully pleads with him.

"Pleeeease. I wanna show you off."

Mike fights a smile but eventually gives in and the two get out of the car.

The salon is carrying on with business as usual. Each booth and section of the salon has a customer in it and the women are hard at work. Music plays. The mimosa flows freely and Denise talks loudly over the music just as Mia and Mike walk in.

When the door closes and the women lay eyes on the couple, the entire place goes silent. The record scratches and the music stops. Everyone looks at them while sharing glances with each other as if an authority figure just walked in. Mike leans over to Mia, whispers.

"What's going on?"

"Not too many men come in here, com'on, relax."

Mia hugs Denise but she playfully pushes her away.

"No, no, no! You're not supposed to be here."

"I know, I know but I gotta get something from the office." Denise doesn't believe her, she knows Mia is up to something but she can't put her finger on it. Mike looks uncomfortable as the women continue working but at the same time giving him side eye looks.

He searches the women's faces, the workers and the customers to ensure they aren't a woman he's been with.

He's more nervous than a mumble rapper at a spelling bee. Mia finishes her conversation with Denise and instructs Mike to follow her to her office. As Mike walks through the shop he can't help but to notice the women are still looking at him snickering and whispering amongst themselves. Mike looks at them suspiciously with each step. When he enters Mia's office he closes the door but can still hear the salon erupt in laughter and the sounds of high-fives.

Mia searches her desk for something.

"What have you been tellin' these women about me?" Mia acts innocent.

"Whatever do you mean, darling?" She flashes a smile while chuckling.

Now Mike knows Mia's been here talking about him, hopefully it's all good.

"Uh-huhq," he responds.

Mia looks up at him smirking, she looks away.

"You know, just a little girl talk. Probably a lot cleaner than what goes on in the barbershop."

She says as she continues to search her desk. Mike brushes it off, leans against the wall with his arms folded. Buried under a stack of paperwork, Mia finds a bracelet. "Here it is," she says, holding it up. "You came here for that?"

"Yeah, I wanna get it cleaned." Mike groans.

"Babe, I woulda just bought you a new one."

Mia gives Mike a "really" look.

"What you gonna do, buy me new jewelry every time something needs to be cleaned?"

"Uhh yeah." Mike responds convincingly.

Mia walks over to him giving Mike a kiss on the cheek. "That's sweet but not fiscally responsible."

Mia exits the office, Mike follows, still trying to convince Mia.

"But we're rich!"

Mia stops walking, turns to Mike. All the eyes and ears in the salon are focused on their conversation.

"Rich is nice, but I wanna be wealthy."

Mike looks around the room trying to understand. He asks, "What's the difference?"

One of the salon workers yells out.

"Another zero!"

The women hoot and holler in solidarity to the claim. They laugh and high-five. Denise chimes in.

"You of all people should know that Mike. You slacking." The women laugh at Denise's comment.

"Ha, Ha, ha. You slipping too, the right side of her hair is uneven."

Denise frantically spins the woman around in the chair looking at both sides of her head also reassuring her she's fine. Mia hits Mike in the arm.

"Leave her alone." Mike shrugs.

"Hey, she came for me first." Denise yells.

"Mia, you better get him outta here before I burn him with this curling iron."

Mia grabs Mike pulling him toward the door.

"See that's why you single, you too violent."

Denise puts down the curling iron, Mia knows Denise is about to say something that would make Mike aware of what she's been doing behind his back. She steps in front of Denise. The two have a non-verbal conversation with just their eyes. Denise nods her head, she stands down.

"I'll see you tomorrow."

Denise responds with sticking her tongue out at Mike like a little kid.

Outside, Mike opens Mia's car door as the two converse. "Why you always gotta get her started?" Mia asks. "Why she always got something smart to say?"

"You know she was just playing buuuut, I mean she didn't say anything wrong. That's something you should know?"

Mike flops in the car embarrassed that he asked that question.

"But why everybody laughed when we went in the office?"

Mia thinks quickly on her feet. She looks down at his crotch.

"Them hooch daddy shorts showing ya print. Maybe you got them excited." Mike looks down and sees his horse print. He confidently smiles.

"Next time I'ma charge'em for the show." Mia laughs, "shut up and let's go. I'm hungry."

Typical for Atlanta, all the good brunch spots are packed. Mia stands in line while Mike takes a ticket from the valet. Mia steps up to the hostess.

"How many?" Mia responds with just two.

The hostess looks over her iPad then tells Mia it's a two-hour wait. She sighs in frustration as Mike walks up standing next to her. He asks her what's wrong, she tells him. Mike turns to the hostess.

"What's your cash app?" The hostess and Mia look at each other confused.

She stammers before giving Mike her cashtag. Mike types on his phone. The money chime sounds on the hostess's phone. She looks at it. Mike sent her $100.

"Now, how long is the wait?" The hostess looks behind her inside the restaurant.

"I have a table being cleaned off right now. I'll be right back."

Mike thanks her as she walks off. Mia looks at Mike lovingly.

"Is there anything you wouldn't do for me?"

"Nope."

The hostess comes back and leads Mike and Mia to their table, dropping menus down in front of them and telling them their server will be with them shortly. Mike and Mia both scan the restaurant pleased with the decor and vibe of the place.

In once section of the restaurant a group of women are thoroughly enjoying their time there. It's clear they're out of towners by the way they're turning up and yelling "Aye" every two seconds. Mia shakes her head annoyed, Mike chuckles at her.

"I mean why do we gotta act like we never been nowhere?" Mia leans over the table asking.

"They probably haven't." The couple stares at them.

"Where do you think they're from?"

Mike gives the group a once over.

"Probably New York or Philly."

"Why those places?" Mike looks at Mia.

"Cause people from New York and Philly barely leave the city. Shit sometimes they never leave their block." Mia laughs, shaking her head.

"Damn Northerners."

"Facts." Mike and Mia laugh.

The two look over their menu. Once Mia decides what she wants she puts it down and announces it to Mike. He still reads through. Mia continues to scan the room then her eyes land on someone. Her heart drops when she makes eye contact with Terry. She lets an "Oh shit" slip out. Mike looks up.

"What?" Mia lies.

"Nothing. Shit, I didn't decide what to drink."

Mia picks up her menu again trying to hide, but it's much too late for that. She looks over the top of it over Mike's shoulder at Terry. Judging by the enormous rock on the woman's finger, Mia concluded that it must be his wife.

Mia looks Allison up and down marveling at her beauty. For a brief second, she got self-conscious. That is until memories of how Terry made her ass clap flooded her brain. She giggles out loud, this time Mike doesn't notice.

She tries not to look at Terry but she can't help it. Butterflies fluttered in her stomach at the sight of seeing him outside of the hotel room even if he is with his wife. She's surprised that her pussy is throbbing. She squeezes her legs closed and looks away from Terry. Mike finally puts his menu down.

"Hey babe, order me the shrimp and grits and a Jameson and ginger." Mike gets up from the table.

"Wh-where are you going." Mike looks down at Mia joking.

"To the bathroom. Why, you wanna come hold it for me?" Mia sticks her tongue out doing a body role.

"Ahhhh don't tempt me."

Mike looks around the restaurant as he leans down to whisper in Mia's ear.

"I dare you." Mia giggles loudly.

It echoes over the music. Her eyes shoot over to Terry who's now looking at her. She covers her mouth then shoos Mike away.

Mike turns around and immediately his eyes land on Allison. He also lets an "oh shit" slip out at the sight of her. He quickly turns around gripping the back of the chair hyperventilating. "Baby, you OK?" Mike nods, and also lies.

"Twisted my knee. Must've turned around too fast."

"Please be careful. I love you but I'm too young and too fine to have a man in a wheelchair." Mike looks at Mia, laughs.

"Oh you got jokes."

"All day baby."

Mike shakes his head then slowly turns around looking at Terry and Allison's table. He thinks to himself. He's sleeping with Terry's wife. Terry from the barbershop. What the hell are the odds. As he walks past their table toward the restroom he avoids eye contact but Allison purposely drops her napkin in front of him.

Mike stops. Freezes, wondering if he should pick it up or not. Should he say something or just put it on the table and keep it moving. Allison made the decision for him.

"Would you mind getting that for me?"

"Uhh, sure."

Mike bends down picking up the napkin. He places it on the table. He and Allison lock eyes.

Terry is too busy looking across the room at Mia to notice the tension between Mike and Allison. Allison smiles at Mike in a way you know there's something between them.

"Thank you," she says in a soft low voice.

Mike gets hard, instantly feeling her warm breath beside his face as he stands. Mike nods then looks over at Terry, he puts on an act.

"Oh snap, Terry! What's good bruh?" Terry turns his attention to Mike, surprised.

"Mike? Oh what's up?" The two dap and hug then stare in an awkward silence for a minute. Then Allison clears her throat. Terry looks at her looking at him.

"Damn, my bad. Mike, this is my wife Allison. Babe, this is Mike. We chop it up sometimes at the barbershop."

Allison extends her hand for Mike to kiss the back of it. He looks back at his table to see Mia watching closely. He opts to shake her hand instead.

"Nice to meet you." Mike points to Mia.

"That's my wife Mia."

Terry and Allison wave, Mia waves back. Mike nervously looks around the restaurant not sure what to say next. "Well, y'all enjoy your brunch. I'm headed to the bathroom." Terry and Allison return the comment to Mike as he walks off.

Inside the restroom, Mike sits in a stall fanning himself. He can feel the heat rise from the back of his neck, the sweat dripping down his back. He thinks that was too close but worries what to do next. Out of all the women in Atlanta, he has to be sleeping with someone he sees every week. Memphis Bleek's song, Is that your Chick, plays over Mike's head from the speakers. He looks up to the ceiling saying out loud, "Really God?"

He spaces side to side in the small stall like a lion in captivity trying to calm himself. Then he stops. Thinks. He knows Allison is a woman in control, she's poised. She wouldn't say anything to Terry let alone Mia so he has nothing to worry about. He hypes himself up by jumping up and down.

Back inside the restaurant, Mia is growing increasingly jealous watching Terry and Allison interact. The way Terry described their relationship is nothing like what they are displaying in public. They are talking, laughing and enjoying each other as if they don't have a care in the world. According to Terry, Allison doesn't spend quality time like this with him, so what the hell is going on? Was everything Terry told her a lie? But it couldn't be. Terry has been so honest, to a fault, about anything Mia's asked him but the math ain't mathin'.

Then Mia catches herself. Oh my god! Has she caught feelings for Terry? Is this why she's jealous? Is this why every time she sees Terry touch Allison's hand or put his hand on her back she's burning inside with rage. I mean they aren't even sitting across from each other, they're sitting side by side. Who does that?

The questions and assumptions about Terry and Allison flood Mia's mind like the mall when the iPhone first came out. She's so preoccupied with her own thoughts and feelings that she drank her drink *and* Mike's drink just to get her emotions under control.

Mike has been sitting at the table for the past two minutes but Mia hasn't noticed. He's talking about something but it all sounds like Charlie Brown to Mia as her gaze on Terry and Allison intensifies. Soon enough, Mike reaches over the table tapping

Mia on her hand. She snaps out of her head and realizes he's back at the table.

"When did you get back?" Mike looks at Mia confused.

"I've been back for a while. Did you drink my drink?"

Mia looks down at the empty glass with lipstick around the rim as evidence.

"Yeah, and it was gross." Mike continues with the questioning.

"Then why'd you drink it?"

Mia looks at Mike annoyed at his line of questioning. "Cause I wanted to see how it tasted."

Mike picks up the glass, signals the server for another one.

"Ummm OK."

Mike studies Mia's face. He knows something is going on. Hell, Ray Charles can see something is eating at Mia. Mike keeps his eyes on hers. If he followed them to what she is looking at he would find out that Mia's mind is on one thing. Terry.

"What's wrong? I got you, just tell me."

Suddenly a calm wave sweeps over Mia. She looks at Mike who is as attentive as he's ever been. She looks down at his hand on hers. Her finger rubs the inside of his hand, he smiles. She took herself back to last night and how she felt about Mike and decided to stay in that feeling.

"Can you sit next to me?" Mike chuckles.

"That's what it is? You want me to sit next to you?" Mia pouts and bats her eyes.

"Yeah. I'm lonely all the way over here and you're all the way over there."

Mike shakes his head thinking Mia is too cute and he loves her vulnerable acting even if it is just to get her way. He slides his chair next to Mia. She rests her head on his shoulder and maintains her focus on him. She doesn't look in Terry or Allison's direction for the remainder of brunch. Instead, she and Mike are in their own world. After a few drinks, the two are laughing and acting like the out-of-town people they made fun of when they first arrived. The turn up was on. At one point Mia started twerking on Mike and received encouragement from most of the women around their table. Why not? After all, it's a Tuesday in Atlanta at one of the best brunch spots in the city. YOLO!

Mike and Mia stayed at Toast on Lenox a lot longer than either of them expected to. Three hours ticked away like minutes. Mia had so much fun she didn't realize Terry and Allison were gone. Mike, able to handle his liquor a lot better than Mia, sat back and encouraged his wife to live her best life and she did. After a brief trip to the bathroom, Mia returned to see Mike talking to the server about the bill. Mike looks confused, Mia thinking she spent too much money, rushes over to try to find out what's happening.

"Something wrong with the bill?" Mike looks at Mia. "Nah. It's already been paid for but the waiter won't tell me who paid it."

Mia throws her arms around Mike's neck pulling him close.

"Who cares. We just ate, drank and turnt up on someone else's dime." Mike bops Mia on the nose.

"You turnt up."

"Yeah but you ate and drank soooo, let's go golfing." Mike's surprised at Mia, she is using his neck to assist her with standing and she thinks she's still going to be able to play golf. Oh this should be a good time, he thinks to himself.

Like most golf courses in America, the one Mike and Mia went to was quiet and white. They look like specs of pepper in a bowl of grits. Of course the older golfers gave them disapproving looks like they should have gone around the back but the younger golfers didn't seem to mind. Mike's real estate firm holds a membership at the club so even if someone wanted to, they couldn't kick them off.

On the golf course, Mia tries her best to focus on hitting the ball but she swings wildly and misses nearly every time. Mike stands behind her watching and snickering. He's more focused on the sway in her hips and the way her skirt snitches on her, she's not wearing any panties.

Unbeknownst to Mike, Mia pre made a drink and put it in a water bottle. He wondered if Mia seemed to become increasingly intoxicated as they moved around the course.

It wasn't until he went to wet his own whistle that he realized there was wine in the bottle. By hole ten all of Mia's golf etiquette went out the window. She randomly yelled, FORE!!! even when she was putting. She ran around the green each time her ball made it in the hole. She's oblivious to the fact that Mike was pushing her ball in when she wasn't looking.

At some point Mia decided to play polo on the golf course. She treated the golf cart like a horse and rode around hitting the ball into different holes.

She interrupted several games. Needless to say, they never made it to the 18th hole. After vomiting into a lake, Mike hoisted Mia over his shoulders and carried her to the car just as the sun was starting to set.

With a rare happy smile on his face, Mike looks over at a sleeping Mia as they drive on the highway. He can't remember the last time they had this much fun together. It was like homecoming all over again. He'd forgotten how much and how fast Mia could let her hair down. When she parties, she *parties*!

Mike looked at Mia so long when he turned his attention back to the highway he had to quickly swerve from running in the back of someone. The car jerking caused Mia to hit her head on the side of the door waking her up. She rubs her head looking around.

"Damn Stevie Wonder. You good?" Mike belts out a loud laugh.

"Wooooow! Stevie tho?"

Mia doesn't respond. She lays back down closing her eyes but then speaks.

"I'm hungry. Can we go to Cookout?" Mike nods his head.

"Oh hell yeah! I want a milkshake."

Mike reaches into a plastic bag pulling out a Body Armor. He hands it to Mia, nudging her on the arm.

"Wake up. Drink this. It'll help and it'll keep the greasy food down."

Mia looks over her shoulder at the bottle then groans as she sits up. She chugs the drink then carelessly tosses the bottle out of the window. Mike can't do anything but laugh and shake his head. Mia doesn't see a problem with what she just did.

"What's the point of having a drop top if you can't do shit like that?" She asked nonchalantly. Mike looks over at her.

"That's not what you do."

"Then what should I do?" Mia asked.

"Oh I can sit on top of the seat. Or flash the cars." Mia goes to lift up her shirt but Mike stops her.

"You are in your bag today. What's gotten into you?" Mia licks Mike's face.

"You. Again tonight hopefully."

Mike cringes at the feeling of spit quickly drying on his face but he doesn't wipe it off.

The next stop of the couple's voyage is the parking lot of Cookout. Being one of the only fast-food places open after nine, there are a line of cars that stretch out onto the street. Mike decided to park and walk up to the window hoping the service would be faster. Mia sits Indian style on the hood of the car admiring Mike and everything about him.

She thought about seeing Terry this morning and was wondering how he felt about seeing her with Mike today. Then it hit her. Mike and Terry know each other. The first thing that came to mind is that this is going to end bad, very bad for everyone involved. Mia's decided, she's going to end things with Terry. After they meet, she has to have one for the road.

Mia shook off that thought. No, it's best to just end it. Cold turkey. Terry is an understanding man, he should be more than OK with her choice. She's thinking of the bigger picture here. It's one thing seeing Terry with his wife but it's another thing knowing that her husband and her sneaky link know each other. Mia checks her phone. No messages from Terry. It's not surprising, they agreed not to text past a particular time. Mia thinks the next four days until she sees Terry again is going to be torture. One moment she hopes he isn't upset with her but then she thinks he wouldn't be. They both knew they were married and what the situation was.

While Mike stood in line, occasionally looking back at Mia, she wonders if Terry is jealous of seeing her with Mike? She wonders if it's the good kind of jealousy that makes a man perform a little better in bed having seen what the other guy looks like. That could be very fun, she thinks to herself.

Incapable of keeping a sensible thought in her mind or standing on whether to break it off with Terry, Mia texts Denise, *I'm coming over*. She jumps, nearly dropping her phone when an old school Chevy Caprice pulls in next to their car blasting Go-Go music. Mia thought to herself, that's an odd combination, but whatever.

Before long, Mike walks over with Mia's food and sits next to her on the hood of the car. She goes straight for the burger, dressing it with cajun fries and BBQ sauce. She ate the double cheesy meat patty in three bites. "I remember these nights," Mike said between sips of his milkshake.

Mia lays back on the hood of the car staring at the stars. The night is clear and there's a slight breeze in the air. With the exception of loud music and the catty voices of drunk people, it's a nice night. Mia responds to Mike thinking about the long nights they've spent in their study group. When they got hungry they'd all march down to the Cookout just outside of campus while someone else made a quick run to insomnia cookies. Those nights helped them survive senior year. Did Mia know Mike cheated on her in college? Of course he did but she didn't care. Honestly, she didn't think the relationship would last past graduation. Mike was moving to Atlanta to start his real estate business and Mia was originally going to Miami to open a salon.

She had no intentions of continuing her relationship with Mike due to his running around. He was supposed to be stable dick in college. But fate had other plans. Mia had come to Atlanta for the Broner Brothers hair show just months before she was to start construction on her salon. While out partying she bumped into Mike and hung out with him all weekend.

It's nights like this that Mike and Mia love. When the city is doing what cities do. People are enjoying themselves and all seems right in the world even for a little while. In those moments they're able to really appreciate the journey they've been on.

Once they've finished eating, Mike and Mia took selfies with each other like high schoolers and posted them on their social media. It's the first picture besides the ones from their wedding they've posted. Mike stands in front of the car holding out his hand. Mia smiles as she takes it. "Let's go home." He says.

"I can't," Mia admits. "I need to go to Denise's."

Mike's at a loss for words. Today has been perfect. The only thing to send if off right is having sex with Mia, preferably the way they had it last night. Now disappointed, Mike decided not to let it show. He merely said OK then helped Mia into the car.

"You're not mad?" She asked, feeling as if she'd just let Mike down. He shakes his head no.

"Nah. I ain't going nowhere."

Mia leans over kissing Mike. Mike chose to make it about Mia for once, he was aware that he doesn't do that too often. So if this is how she wanted to spend part of her evening, then he was fine with it.

Denise sits on the edge of her sofa shoving caramel popcorn in her mouth hanging on to Mia's every word. Mia spaces around the living recounting running into Terry and his wife at the Toast of Lenox. You would think Mia was telling Denise what went down on Epstein's island the way she was tuned in.

Mia explains the story with anger and concern in her voice. It had been bothering her all day which is the reason why she decided to drink the way she did earlier that day. She used alcohol as a way to mask her feelings so that Mike wouldn't inquire about her behavior. She tried not to think about it but she couldn't so she took it out with her antics on the golf course. Denise's eyes bug out as she hang on Mia's every word.

"He acted like he didn't even know me."

Denise turns her face up looking at Mia trying to understand why she's so upset.

"I mean what was he supposed to do? Introduce you as the smell on his dick?"

Denise laughs loud at her own joke but Mia isn't amused at all. She throws a pillow at Denise knocking the popcorn out of her hand. It spills all over the floor in front of her but it doesn't stop her laugh. Mia flops down the sofa putting her face in her hands, her words muffled as she speaks.

"I don't know what's happening. Mike and I had such a great day planned and it started off great then this."

Denise bends over picking up the popcorn offering her take on the situation.

"Listen M, he did what he was supposed to do and his wife or Mike didn't know a thing. You can continue doing what you're doing. I don't see the big deal."

Mia looks up, giving Denise an ugly look.

"I think I'm falling for Terry, that's the big deal. Why else would I be jealous." Denise sits next to Mia holding her hand. She looks her in the eyes the way only a true friend could.

"It's because you gave a piece of yourself to him. We do that during sex. The problem is we think we own these people, we think we own that exchange of energy and passion exclusively but we don't. We are supposed to enjoy the people we have for as long as we can and that's it."

Mia hears what Denise is saying but she's not in the emotional state to rationalize the legitimacy of her words. Instead of taking Denise's words to heart, she challenges them knowing Denise would feel the same if the shoe was on the other foot.

"So if you walked into the shop and I was drinking mimosas with Ashley, you wouldn't feel some type of way??"

Denise jumps up ready to fight.

"I'll beat yo ass!" Mia nods her head, it's exactly what she thought Denise would say.

"Ashley ain't as close to you as I am so why would you be in our shop drinking mimosas with her? She don't even work there."

Mia believes she's proved her point and her feelings are justified.

"See, it's the same thing." Denise disagrees.

"But it's not, Ashley is a friend-," Mia interrupts. "Yeah but I've known her longer than you."

Denise holds her hand up for Mia to stop talking, that's not what she wants to hear and she knows Mia is deflecting.

"You've known her longer but you and me have been through the trenches together. Terry was with his wife. A woman he's been through some real shit with. You might not wanna hear this but you are the second course entree, his wife is the main course. You don't have the right to feel some type of way."

Mia looks at Denise with her face turned up.

"Bitch did you just call me a salad?" Mia smacks her own butt.

"You see this ass? I'm a steak. Tomahawk!" Denise exhales from exhaustion.

"Point is what you and Terry have or had or whatever is what helped you be better with Mike and ya'll are in a good place, right? OK so the hell with your feelings. Keep getting your itch scratched by Terry so you can go home and be the happy wife you've been."

Mia sits with her thoughts for a moment as Denise's words break through her anger and feeling of being rejected. She looks at Denise then bends down helping her clean up the rest of the popcorn.

"You're right. I just wasn't prepared to see him with her or any other woman for that matter. Terry doesn't exist outside the hotel room and that made it easy to deal with that's all."

Denise leaves the room throwing a handful of popcorn in the trash. She returns with an open bottle of wine then refreshes their glasses.

"I get it, I do. But you knew what he was when you started. So what you gonna do now?" Mia gulps down the wine to Denise's surprise.

"First I'ma get her face outta my head and keep it G. I'll be OK."

Denise looks at Mia as if she doesn't believe her.

"What happens if you can't do that the next time you're with Terry?"

Mia thinks as she pours the rest of the wine in her glass.

"I'll cover his face with a pillow." Denise laughs and the women high-five each other.

On the uber ride home Mia stares at her phone looking down at an open blank text message she's contemplating on sending to Terry. The time on the phone reads 11:11 p.m. Knowing the power of numbers, Mia closes the text, closes her eyes and says an affirmation to herself. The driver looks at her in the rearview mirror at her whispering to herself.

She questions what her next move should be after replaying Denise's words in her mind. She wasn't trying to get Denise to shut up when she told her she was right, about everything. The time she's spent with Terry was exactly what she needed and it is undoubtedly helping her and Mike have a better relationship. She no longer wondered where Mike was or what he was doing and with whom.

She is doing something that brought her closer to her husband and thought maybe what Mike was doing was making her draw closer to her. Turns out she just needed a reality check and it worked. She had a short lapse in judgment but she's good now. Terry is married and despite what he told her, she of all people knows how fast a relationship can go from good to bad and vice versa. With that, all is right again.

Mia walks into the quiet house assuming Mike is asleep and she starts kicking herself. She was so wrapped up in seeing Terry with his wife that she ruined the day she had planned with Mike. They never made it to getting her bracelet cleaned and she had planned on having a repeat of last night, now that moment has passed.

Frustrated with her behavior, she slowly walks upstairs thinking of what she's going to do for the rest of the night. She reaches the top of the stairs and turns the corner to see Mike about to put his hand on the doorknob of the linen closet where she's hidden her cheating gifts. Quickly she rushes over, blocking Mike from opening the door.

"Hey, what you doing?"

Mike looks at Mia chuckling not sure why she's denying him entry.

"I thought you were asleep."

"Nah I didn't know how long you'd be gone so I was gonna shower and wait up for you."

Mia runs her index finger down the center of Mike's bare chest licking her lips.

"You was gonna wait up for me?" Mike watches Mia's hand inch its way to his waist.

"Yeah I wanted to take full advantage of that liquor in your system." Mia giggles.

"You know what they say. Tequila is nasty but after a few shots, so am I."

Mike hoists Mia in the air, she wraps her legs around his waist and her arms around his neck.

"Exactly," Mike says, then he kisses Mia.

"I think we should make a movie tonight." Mike's eyes widen.

He's shocked and surprised. Mia looks down between her legs feeling Mike's erection.

"I'ma take that as a yes. Go get in the shower, I'll set up the tripod."

"We don't need towels." Mike smiles nodding his head yes as he carries Mia into the bedroom.

Chapter 7

Men are in the barbershop, some getting their haircut others awaiting their turn.

Sports plays on silent on the TV's as music fills the air. Mike enters the barbershop with a big smile on his face. His barber sees him and greets him with an enthusiastic, "Whaddup!"

Mike sits down in the awaiting chair as the barber throws the cape around him just as another customer was about to sit down. The barber addresses him.

"I'll be with you after my man right here." The man isn't happy but he nods then sits back down without saying a word.

"What's been going on with'chu Mike?"

"Shiiit, I can't call it." The barber laughs.

"You got it. So what you knockin' off this week?" Mike joins in the laugh as he speaks.

"Maaaan. I've been just with one chick for the past few months." The barber looks at Mike with disbelief.

"Say what? So it's just you and wife now huh." Mike shakes his head no.

"Nah, I got this married woman named,"

The men in the barbershop erupt in WHOAAAA's stopping Mike from continuing further.

"Whoa, whoa, no names bruh you know that. We have plausible deniability in here." Mike chuckles again. "You right, you right. But yeah, this married woman is something out of a Comic-con. I mean it's like having sex with a different person every time. The costumes, the voices, the sex is always different. I cut off all my other hoes for this one."

The men in the shop laugh, Mike looks around trying to get in on the joke. His barber says, "Look at this man cheating monogamously." The men laugh again, another barber chimes in.

"He is more faithful to the side piece. I smell a divorce comin'."

Mike immediately disagrees with that statement as he has no plans of divorcing Mia, it's never crossed his mind. "Nah, nothing like that. But it's weird tho cause ever since I started hittin' off the married broad, Mia been different."

The men react as if they know trouble is on the horizon. A patron asks, "What do you mean different?" Mike takes a moment to gather his thoughts.

"She don't be goin' through my phone no more, I got food cooked every night, no naggin', no attitude. It's like she know but don't care. And we having really, really good sex."

The men in the shop look around avoiding eye contact with Mike. Then the two barbers blurt out, "SHE CHEATIN!" Everyone silently nods in agreement. Mike shifts in the barber chair uncomfortably. He doesn't want to believe it but it hits him, if someone else would have said what he just said, his first thought would be the same. But he knows Mia, she's not for the streets, she's never been so he can confidently sit back and reject their claim.

"Nah it ain't that."

Everyone disagrees with Mike. His barber tries to convince him that he's not seeing the writing on the wall. He explains when a woman acts like she doesn't care or something doesn't bother her that means she's either creeping around or is already talking to a divorce attorney. Another barber jokes that she's about to take half his money and run off with his best friend. Mike's face tells everyone what he's feeling.

"Don't gas me up 'cause it's gonna be a lot of slow singin' and flower bringin' if her cell phone starts ringin.'"

The men agree with Mike's Biggie reference. One man gets up and gives him dap for it. Then an awkward silence falls over the shop. Mike's ego won't allow the words of the men to show it bothers him but now a bunch of things are running through Mike's mind. Is Mia capable of cheating on him? Has he pushed her to the brink of stepping out on him after the numerous times he's done it. The rational part of him understands that if she did, she is more than justified. However, the primal man inside of him is feeling a small sense of fear of the possibility.

While lining the side of Mike's face, his barber can see Mike's eyes stare in a daze. He turns the clippers off and leans down to his ear whispering, "Pay attention to the changes in your woman especially if you haven't made any changes toward her."

Mike thinks as those words echo in his mind. He decides to get real candid with his barber.

"Maybe I'm getting older or maybe I'm just tired of the sneaking around, lying and living a double life but I always knew Mia is the one I'm supposed to be with. I think it's finally hittin' me. She's all I want."

The Barber steps back, looks at Mike proudly. Mike turns around looking at the barber with an inquisitive face. The barber nods his head like a proud father.

"I'm proud of you." Mike chuckles, not sure what to make of the comment.

"Proud of me for what?"

"Cause now you're thinking like a grown man."

The barber says, continuing lining Mike.

"Yeah but what I'ma do about the sex? This married woman? Lawd! She's every type of freak I've ever had or wanted all rolled up as one woman. Mia could never be that."

His barber looks at him with a stern face and says, "It ain't always about the sex. What Mia lacks, she makes up in other ways. You gotta finally realize what they are." The barber pats Mike on the shoulders.

After his line up, Mike sits in the car thinking about the things that were discussed while getting his hair cut. In his mind he combs over the last few months and the sudden changes Mia has made toward him. Had he missed the signs of Mia potentially cheating? Is she being the freak Allison is being for him for someone else?

154

The thought of Mia with another man turns Mike's stomach and he becomes nauseas. The faces and bodies of all the women he's slept with flash in his mind like a pornhub compilation video. Then somewhere while that is happening, the faces of the women turn to the faces of men that could have been with Mia.

Mike quickly opens the car door and vomits onto the pavement. He sweats. He hears his heart beating rapidly. He thinks he's having a panic attack. He tears his shirt off and fans himself with it while turning the car AC on full blast. The cool air blows on Mike's bare chest as he reclines his chair trying to slow his breathing.

The world Mike's created in his mind has just closed in on him after one conversation. The realization has set in that he could have unknowingly pushed Mia into the arms of another man. As a result, that man or men, is the reason for Mia's change in behavior.

After ten minutes, Mike has calmed himself into a place he can think more clearly. He's decided there's no point in working himself up into a frenzy over hypothetical scenarios, he's going to find out for himself. He frantically searches for his phone that fell down between the middle console of the car. He types a business name into the map then cranks the car and speeds off.

Mike sits in the waiting room of a posh lawyer's office nervously tapping his knee. Before long, a secretary approaches Mike.

"You can go in now."

Mike leaps to his feet and follows the secretary into an office. Mike shakes hands with a heavy set balding Jewish attorney who greets him with a jovial voice.

"Micheal! Happy to see you, you're looking well. What brings you in today? Have a seat."

Mike declines taking a seat as he's too worked up to sit down, he really only came in to ask one question.

"Has Mia contacted you recently or some time in the recent past?"

The lawyer looks at Mike perplexed as he sits at his desk.

"Well yes, she has. A month ago."

Mike stares at the lawyer as if his answer is going to change. The two look at each other and the lawyer can feel something is wrong with Mike and takes his concern seriously. Mike's eyes widened.

His worst fears have just been confirmed by the lawyer. A large piece of him wanted the answer to be no but it's obviously not the case. Shit just got real for Mike. He paces around the room hitting the side of his head. His barber and all the men in the shop were right. She's thinking about divorce. Shit, shit, shit. Now what.

"OK, what are my options here? How can I protect myself?" The lawyer now looks utterly confused.

"Protect yourself against what?"

Mike stops pacing and slams his hands on the desk yelling, "THE DIVORCE!"

The lawyer takes a beat then starts to laugh. Mike is not amused. At. All. He swipes the items off the desk, sending them flying against the wall and crashing onto the floor. The lawyer becomes frightened. He jumps to his feet trying to defuse Mike's anger.

"Wait! Wait! Wait! She didn't talk to me about a divorce!" he yells out.

Mike immediately stops his tirade. He stares at the scared lawyer with fire in his eyes.

"What?" The lawyer repeats himself.

"She didn't talk about a divorce."

Mike blinks several times trying to compute the words. The lawyer informs Mike that Mia came into his office a month ago to talk to him about making Denise a partner in the second salon. She wanted the paperwork drawn up so she can present it to Denise on her birthday next month.

Mike is stunned. He realizes he's overreacted, big time. The lawyer looks at him hoping his revelation is calming Mike down. It is. Mike looks at him, remorse and calmness on his face.

"She came to you about her business? Not about us?"

The lawyer slowly walks around his desk looking Mike square in the eye and says no. Mike exhales deeply then flops down into the chair. He smiles to himself, the lawyer continues to look at him not sure of the meaning of Mike's questioning.

"Is everything OK?" He asks.

Mike looks out the window gazing at the Atlanta skyline. Mike nods his head yes.

"My wife isn't thinking about divorce."

The lawyer sits on the edge of his now cleared desk with his hands folded in his lap.

"Legally, I can confidently say, your marriage is fine."

Mike laughs to himself out loud, the lawyer smiles. Mike apologizes to the lawyer then starts picking the items littering the office floor. The lawyer tells him he doesn't have to do that but Mike insists anyway.

It's the least he can do. Once he's done, Mike looks down at the carnage, some things were broken in the process.

"Replace anything I broke out of my retainer." The lawyer chuckles and extends his hand.

"Already done." Mike and his lawyer shake hands and share a laugh.

Later, Mike walks through a rental property that has just been finished being rehabbed. He talks with his appraiser and contractor at all the details that were incorporated in the design and is pleased at the work. While the appraiser discusses what the house can go on the market for, Mike's thoughts are on Mia.

While he's relieved to find out that Mia is not thinking about getting a divorce, he can't help to wonder if she's cheating. He could deal with a divorce, not saying it wouldn't hurt but he could live with her leaving. But he is finding it extremely difficult to get over her giving her body to a man. Part of it is ego but the main part of it is that he knows how men think.

He knows when a man sleeps with a woman who is in a relationship that man doesn't view the woman with the best intentions in his mind. A man sees that woman as a toy he can use and not care about her feelings or pleasure and typically has nasty thoughts about her while doing nasty things with her. Mia is his delicate flower and her body should be handled with care and not a sperm bank.

Mike dodged the first bullet with the lawyer but finding out if Mia is cheating is going to be a little more tricky to navigate. He's going to have to do things women typically do to find out but he's determined to find out. He's going to have to be cautious when doing it. If Mia finds out he may have to answer questions he's not ready to answer. He may have to tell Mia about Allison if it comes to that. Mike believes Mia may not be able to move past him being with Allison when she learns it's been a consistent thing.

That might be the straw to break the horse's back because being with Allison sounds more like a relationship than just casual sex regardless of what their arrangement is. Nevertheless, Mike is going to get to the bottom of his suspicions tonight.

At home, Mike silently pulls into the driveway of his house. He parks his car next to Mia's and looks up at the windows. He sees a single light on in their bedroom and thinks Mia may still be awake. When he gets out of the car he's careful to shut the car door without it making a sound. He then creeps over to Mia's car. Looking through the window he can see she left the doors unlocked. Carefully he opens it occasionally looking up at the bedroom window to ensure Mia isn't looking.

Mike searches the car, not sure of what he's looking for but anything that would show signs of her cheating. The passenger seat looks like it hasn't been reclined. He smells the seat and it still has the new car smell suggesting no one may have sat in it. The driver's seat is close enough to the steering wheel consistent with how short she is. Mike safely assumes she hasn't had another man driving the car. He continues with his search however the glove box, center console, backseat pockets and trunk all turn up empty. He hasn't found a gift, hotel receipt, a change of clothes or anything. But to Mike, that still doesn't mean anything, he will continue looking for clues.

Mike finds Mia asleep on top of the covers. She's in a sexy purple lingerie set, her hair is done and she's posed in a seductive manner. Mike watches her sleep as his eyes trace every curvature of her body. On the pillow next to her Mike sees a small folded note with her lipstick on the top of it.

He ignores the note at first and tip toes to the nightstand, looking down at Mia's phone. He keeps his eyes on Mia as he very slowly and quietly reaches for her phone. Finally he gets it. Mike sits on the opposite side of the bed with his back to Mia as he goes through her text messages.

He finds nothing. Then he checks her internet history. Her photos then locations. He finds nothing. He breathes a sigh of relief then looks over at Mia.

He returns his attention to the note. Picks it up, opens it. Reads. Wake me up and tell me to do whatever you want. XO XO. Mike thinks. He's been overreacting, Mia isn't cheating. She's always at home like a good woman just waiting for him to arrive and show her the man she married.

Mike closes the note, looks at Mia again before putting the note back on the pillow. He takes out his phone, sits it on the nightstand. Then he puts Mia's phone back on the nightstand. Mike looks at Mia tenderly. He thinks about everything he's put Mia through these past six years and concluded that enough is enough. The thought of Mia cheating on him is enough for him to realize he has everything he wants laying right beside him. It's always been clear to him that Mia would do anything he asks if she knew it'll make him happy. Well, almost everything, polyamory is still out of the question. Point is, he never really gave Mia the opportunity to do the things he would like.

It's not like she hasn't asked but it always came from a place of conceding. She would offer to do the things he was getting from other women when they argued or when he was caught cheating. To Mike it feels like she would only do it to keep him away from other women. That feeling made him feel like he was being controlled and manipulated. It didn't seem like it came from a place of her actually wanting to do it on her own.

But again, he's never told her what he liked or wanted to try. Subsequently, he's never asked her either. They've never talked about their sexual fantasies. They both assumed that having sex with each other was enough. But after nearly 12 years together, people's tastes change. Things get stale and some new energy is needed.

It makes Mike wonder is that why he cheated in the first place? Is Mia not sexually open enough? How would he know? Truth be told, Mike's cheating has nothing to do with what Mia isn't doing. Mike hasn't matured. He is still stuck in his high school and college mentality where he could have any woman he wanted whenever he wanted. Being handsome and athletic with money afforded Mike to be desired by so many women. It's been like that his entire life. It's one hell of an ego boost, a constant rush of adrenaline that soon became as addictive as likes to an Instagram model. It's something very difficult to let go when that's all you've known your whole life. The immaturity in him wouldn't allow him to be faithful in fear of missing out. Mike asked himself, really, what is he missing out on? Pussy, ass and tits are everywhere, they just look different but the end result is the same. You cum and do it all over again. Outside of the conquest and spoils of the hunt Mike came to the realization that it's not that serious.

While he undressed and wrestled with his newfound insight on his behavior, a thought entered his mind and it's as clear as if God himself spoke the words. He's going to break it off with Allison and for the first time be completely committed to Mia. She deserves it but more importantly, Mike is making the choice to be a better man for himself and his wife.

The decision came easy and was met without a second thought or any type of opposition. He is going to stop cheating but not tell Mia about Allison. Instead, he's committed to being transparent with Mia about his sexual needs. Who knows, Mia may like the idea of dressing up like an anime character or power ranger. It might be something new and exciting for her as well.

The only fear Mike has is his truth being rejected or worse, ridiculed. Black women typically don't do the outside the box type of stuff. However, if he's going to let go of his boyish ways, he has to find out just what Mia is willing to embrace. In return, he will do the same for her. He's willing to deal with the embarrassment or the reaction from Mia because she's worth more.

As he lays in the bed next to Mia still sleeping peacefully he affirmed to himself that if Mia didn't go with what he would soon tell her, he would be OK with it and he will not go elsewhere. If all else fails, there's always porn.

Mike looks over at Mia's butt poking toward him. He licks his lips at the sight of her panties wedged between her smooth soft butt cheeks and smiles to himself. He's got one hell of a woman. Instead of pulling her panties to the side and waking Mia up with his tongue he chose to cuddle next to her.

Mike wraps his arms around her waist, tightly, pulling her close and burying his face in her hair. He puts one hand on one of Mia's breasts and enjoys the scent of warm vanilla and honey as it pleasantly invades his nostrils. He then whispers in her ear.

"I love you and I'm going to do better. I promise. It's just me and you from now on."

Mike leans over giving her a kiss on the forehead before closing his eyes.

At the same time, Mia opens her eyes with a smile. She's been awake the entire time. She knew he arrived when the car headlights shined through the bedroom window. Like he'd done the night before, she waited up for him. She felt the forehead kiss and heard every word. Each syllable is like music to her ears, the best melody ever.

She lays in the bed feeling Mike's strong arms around her waist and warm chest on her back thinking to herself. Who knew? Who knew an affair could help Mike see what he's had at home all this time. This wasn't the plan but Mia is definitely going to take the win. It's all she's ever wanted, for him to be better, for him to want to be better. And it seems like it's working.

The past three days have been some of the best between them in a very long time and is evidence of the years to come if he stays the course. With Mike's admission, Mia now has to do something she didn't think she'd have to do this soon. Break it off with Terry. When the affair with Terry started, Mia thought when the time came to break it off it would be easy. Now, she's not so sure.

Terry came to her during a time she was nearly broken and he helped pull her out of a dark place. Terry is more than a lover to Mia, he's a friend and confident. The type of friend Denise could never be. Remembering Terry's friend analogy, it now resonates with her more.

It feels almost like a betrayal to end things despite them both knowing it would eventually. An uneasy feeling swept over Mia during her thoughts. She feels like she used Terry, like he was a placeholder until the real Mike finally decided to show up. Despite her feeling of dread, the end goal is a successful marriage with Mike. It isn't like Mia's the first woman Terry has been with and he is still married. Not only is Mia convinced he will understand, she's certain Terry will find someone else.

Mia's still not sure of Terry's feelings for her, or if he has any outside of the hotel room. She is not completely sure how Terry will take the sudden cease to their fling. She hopes he doesn't ask a bunch of questions but one thing is clear, she doesn't want him to think it's because she saw him with his wife. The last thing Mia wants is to have Terry's last memory of her to be that of a jealous woman.

Before finally falling asleep in marital bliss, Mia tossed around the idea of sleeping with Terry one last time before cutting things off. She's thought about this before. If she's going to go cold turkey, then one last hot and sweaty sexcapade would be a good parting gift to them both. Her at her most sexy would be the thought she'd want to leave Terry with. Why not?

Mia stands in the middle of her shop signing for a delivery while from the corner of her eye she watches Denise flirt with the delivery guy. She rolls her eyes when she's done signing and patiently waits for him to finish putting his number in Denise's phone. Then he turns his attention to Mia taking the tablet from her.

"Thank you."

Mia simply nods while giving him a look. She stands next to Denise as they watch him leave out.

"Do you have to flirt with every man that comes in here?" Mia asks. Denise looks at her as if she's been insulted.

"Not every man, I didn't flirt with Mike the other day, did I?" Mia shakes her head while sorting through the boxes.

"You gon' stop talkin' 'bout my husband." Denise waves her finger in Mia's face.

"I would but you keep bringin' him up and that nonsense he said last night, when he thought you were sleepin'. You can't really be tellin' me you believe him."

Mia gives Denise an of course she does look... Denise scoffs, rolling her eyes.

"You know he only said that because you was naked, right?" Mia laughs it off.

"I wasn't naked. I was naked adjacent."

"What the hell is naked adjacent? I see you just makin' up stuff now."

Mia and Denise share a laugh. Mia doesn't even know why she talks to Denise about Mike. All of her advice or comments are always going to be on the opposite. Denise is anti-Mike, just like her mother and she doubts it will ever change. Denise hops on the counter next to where Mia is working.

"Please tell me you're not gonna take one last ride before leaving Terry land. You need to make a clean break."

"I thought about it but I'ma take one more lap around the track then go."

Mia responds. Denise doesn't approve. She exhales then begins to help Mia. A loud sound of thunder shakes the salon windows. The lights flicker on and off and the women in the salon react afraid. Rain starts to downpour.

Denise looks outside the windows. It's dark and the rain is coming down like a monsoon. She turns to Mia.

"See, God don't like ugly." Mia looks at her playfully pouting.

"I know. I'll ask him if I can visit you in hell."

Denise is taken aback by Mia's quick comeback. She throws a bundle of hair at her unable to verbally return the jab. Mia looks down at her watch. It's almost time for her to meet Terry. She walks to the window looking out at the water filling the sides of the streets and thinks to herself, maybe this is an omen. Maybe Denise is right. Maybe she should rock Terry's world then leave him holding his own nuts.

Truth is, Mia is better off just giving Terry a call or leaving a note at the front desk. Because she knows if she goes to the hotel and sees him, clothes are coming off. As the rain beats on the windows Mia is unable to hear Denise talking behind her. Moments later, she can hear Denise clearly.

"Uh, what did you say?" Denise stands beside Mia looking out at the weather do its thing.

"I said maybe you should take an Uber. You know Atlanta drivers act crazy when it rains."

Mia thinks about the option for a second but she doesn't want to wait to get away from Terry after she tells him. She kisses Denise on the cheek.

"I'll be fine."

Rain continues to pour down on the city as Terry arrives at the hotel. He exits his car, covering his head from the rain then gives the keys to the valet before running into the hotel lobby. The hotel is in full chaos. There's a long line leading up to the front desk full of angry guests. People yell and complain as the receptionist struggles to keep order. Terry skips past the line and goes right up to the desk.

People complain and yell at him for cutting ahead but he ignores them. The receptionist sees Terry and gets more flustered. He looks around the counter at a stack of hotel room keys. He picks up one and hands it to Terry then goes back to calming down the crowd. Terry chuckles as he heads to the elevator.

Just as the elevator doors close Mike shuffles through the crowd and enters the hotel as well. He impatiently stands behind the sea of people crowding the receptionist desk smacking his teeth. He waves at the receptionist until he finally gets his attention. The receptionist slides a hotel key card on the edge of the counter then nods to Mike.

Mike bypasses the upset people grabbing the key but leaving a hundred-dollar bill in the key card spot. He looks around ensuring no one recognizes him as he heads to the elevator. On the elevator Mike exhales, he looks nervous. Like Mia plans to do with Terry, Mike came to the hotel to break things off with Allison. He just hopes she doesn't have some new sexy costume because he's not sure he can trust himself not to put his hand in the cookie jar one last time.

Just as Mike exits the elevator, the lights in the hotel flicker on and off. They stay off for a minute making the hotel hallway eerily quiet and spooky. Mike knows exactly where he's going but walks down the hallway with caution anticipating a monster to jump out on him. Finally he makes it to the room but the power in the hotel is still out and his key card won't work. Mike continues to try the door until the lights come back on and he's granted access inside.

Meanwhile, Mia drives down the street struggling to see the road as the rain pounds on the windshield while nervously talking to herself. She rehearses what she's going to say to Terry but no matter what she says, nothing sounds right.

"Terry, I just wanna say thank you for the many, many, many orgasms. No, don't start with that. But Terry, soooo we can't do this anymore. No, no it's not you. It's me. I wanna work on my marriage. But if he acts up again, I'ma call you."

Mia smacks her forehead for sounding like a bad 90's rom-com breakup scene. She repeatedly tells herself to get it together, this shouldn't be that hard. She looks at herself in the rearview mirror and tries again, this time sounding like Denzel Washington in Training Day.

"Aye bruh. We had fun. It's over. Don't call me. What? No? I said what I said. You don't want this smoke."

As Mia gets closer to the hotel she feels a pit in her stomach. She thought there would be more traffic on the way there giving her more time to go over her breakup speech. She has to keep reminding herself that it's not a breakup, they aren't in a relationship. It's a good-bye speech. Yeah, that works. This is good-bye. Have a nice life. It was fun. There! She got it. That's what she's going to say. She'll keep it short and sweet. The jury is still on the sex part though.

A flash of lightning rips through the sky followed by a loud boom then the roar of thunder. She looks toward the sky from the windshield thinking God is trying to tell her something. But she continues driving until she makes it to the hotel valet.

One of the valets holds an umbrella over Mia's head as he walks her into the hotel. She's met with the same scene Mike and Terry were met with but she waits her turn at the back of the line. The receptionist looks up and makes eye contact with Mia. The look on his face says not you too but he reluctantly signals for Mia to come to the front.

In front of him but off to the side are two hotel keys. He slides one to Mia while the unruly crowd gets more and more upset. He tries to calm them down saying he's waiting for the computers to come back online. When someone questions why Mia got a key he tells them she's already checked in and this key is an extra one he didn't give her earlier.

The people give Mia dirty looks but she already has enough on her mind to let it get to her. She keeps rehearsing her short speech to herself as she heads toward the elevator. A bell boy stops her just as she presses the up button.

"Ma'am, the power has been acting up. I would hate for you to get stuck, maybe you should take the stairs."

The stairs?! Mia thinks to herself. The room she and Terry share is on the eighth floor. The bell boy shrugs telling Mia it's her choice as he walks away. Not needing to have Terry think she stood him up if she gets stuck on the elevator, she heeds the bell boy's warning and takes the stairs.

Then the last piece of the love cube, Allison arrives rolling a suitcase behind her. She hasn't spoken to Mike but seeing him with his wife ignited a fire inside of her and she's been anxiously anticipating their weekly meetup. She can see why Mike is cheating on Mia. Allison didn't see anything special about her, she looks like a basic wife. Although Allison doesn't view Mia in the same erotic league as her, she still is going to put on a performance that will have him thinking about her even when he's with Mia.

She has something special in store for Mike today and she's sure it's going to blow his mind. When she enters the hotel she too is surprised by the chaos in the lobby but she's not about to stand in anyone's line. Ignoring all the people in front of the desk, she walks right up to it and grabs the key card knowing exactly where it is.

A flash of lightning illuminates the lobby followed by another roar of thunder that shakes the entire hotel. She waits by the elevator, rainwater drips off her long tan Burberry trench coat. Her eyes don't leave the numbers descending from the top of the elevator. Finally the door dings and opens, Allison steps off standing with her back to the wall. As the doors close, a woman runs toward the elevator. She yells for Allison to hold it open but she doesn't move. The doors close on the woman just as she reaches them. Allison giggles to herself. The only thing on her mind is Mike and today is special for Allison as well because thunderstorms turn her on. She can hardly wait for the elevator to stop on her floor.

The stairway is hot and as Mia goes up each flight of stairs Mia sweats more. Instead of going over her speech in her head she focuses on making it to the floor. She rejoices inside when she has one flight to go. When she reaches the top, she takes a minute to rest against the door catching her breath. After she does, she uses her phone camera to check her appearance. She fixes her hair, does an armpit check then adjusts her clothes before exiting the stairwell. In the hallway, the lights flicker on and off again scaring Mia just a little. The feeling of a bad omen sweeps over her body again. She stops walking. Mia stands in the middle of the quiet hallway thinking if she should continue or just turn around and go back to her salon.

The thing that stops her is when she puts herself in Terry's shoes. How would she feel if he didn't show up and was never heard from again? She'd be pissed and feel rejected. That feeling would stay with her until she got some type of closure. Mia doesn't want to put Terry through that, he deserves better. She continues walking until she reaches the door. Mia hesitates putting the key card into the slot.

Mike paces around the hotel room checking his watch thinking Allison is normally so punctual but she's late today. He looks out of the hotel room window at the dark sky and rain beating on the window. Then the lights go out again. This time, they don't turn back on. He tries the light switch but they don't turn on. Mike shrugs it off then takes off his shirt, pants, hops into bed.

The room is nearly pitch black when he hears the keycard swipe and the door opens. He sees the silhouette of a woman in the doorway. Yes! She's finally here. Mike tries to think about what they're going to do today but his mind goes in a million ways. He watches her stand there for a minute, Mike smiles awaiting what's to come next. The door closes and she slowly walks toward the bed.

Mia enters the dark room. As she walks toward the bed she sees Terry's silhouette in the bed. She points her phone flashlight on the silhouette, but he holds his hand up blocking the light. Mia quickly puts the phone down whispering, "Oops." Mia turns the flashlight off.

She exhales before dropping her purse on the desk. No one says a word. Mia is still struggling with coming out with it or getting into the bed. She stares at him laying in the bed and watches his erection point up through the sheets. She immediately gets moist and that's all the confirmation she needs. She's going to fuck him then dump him.

Mia pushes her anxiety of having to break things off with him aside then slowly undresses. She stands at the foot of the bed as nervous as she was the first time she was in the room with Terry. She trembles a little bit but he can't see. She reaches for her phone putting on a slow R&B song. Mia exhales then seductively crawls onto the bed and on top of him. They start kissing.

Moments into the kiss, Mia feels strange. There's something familiar about kissing Terry. She ignores it thinking it's her body's way of telling her she made the right choice. He goes to say something but Mia puts her finger over her lips. He stops what he was going to say then grabs her by the back of the head bringing her closer to him. They kiss deeply, passionately then wildly.

This feels different to Mia. Terry has never been aggressive and has never shown this much passion when they were together. It turns Mia on. His hand slides between her legs gently inserting 2 fingers. He slowly massages in and out making Mia instantly squirt all over his hands. It's so intense that Mia grabs him by the neck pushing him back as she rides his fingers with pure enjoyment. With her free hand she yanks his hands out of her bringing them to her lips. She tastes herself licking his fingers clean while she grinds on his shaft. This is new for him as well. Having Mia taste herself was hot and he wondered if she likes the taste so much would she like the taste of another woman as well. In an effort not to ruin the moment he says nothing.

Mia puts his hands on her hips allowing him to control her slow grind. She feels herself dripping over his dick smiling at the sound it makes. Then she turns around reverse cowgirl, he smacks her ass hard, it echoes over the music. Mia slides back sitting on his face then puts him in her mouth.

They give each other FaceTime, Mia smothering his face with her soaking lips while trying not to choke with all of him in her mouth. She grips his legs to keep her position steady but the sensation feels too good. She matches her bobbing with the rhythm of his tongue strokes. He grabs two handfuls of her ass as her wetness floods his face. The feeling of her warm mouth as it grips him is almost too much for him to take.

At the same time, Allison blindfolds and gags Mike despite him putting up a little opposition. Eventually he goes with it knowing she wouldn't take no for an answer. Allison then uses a silk scarf to tie both his hands together before dressing up in a full leather outfit.

Through the darkness, she searches through the suitcase until she finds a vibrator. She turns it on. The sound of it makes Mike nervous, but he doesn't move. Allison snatches the sheets off him, the cold air hits his body making him shiver. She then massages his manhood with the vibrator. He moans from the sensation.

Allison then puts the vibrator in her mouth then performs oral sex. He tries his best not to cum but it gets increasingly difficult. Moments later he can't take it anymore and lets loose. She giggles but doesn't stop causing him to shake and squirm. Through the gag he tries to talk but no words escape. Allison enjoys the reaction.

Chapter 8

Later while the room is still dark and the sounds of rain and wind beat on the nearby window, Mia and Terry are breathing heavily. Mia talks in between breaths.

"Baby. Not that I'm complaining. But it ain't never been this good before. Whew."

Mia's voice sounds eerily familiar to him. He touches her face, her hair then her breasts as she giggles. The laugh. The laugh is a dead giveaway. His heart begins to beat rapidly. Could this really be happening?

Mia thinks he's ready to go again but she knows this is supposed to be the last time. With her body fully relaxed still reeling from the multiple orgasms, Mia comes out with what she came here to tell him.

"But I have to tell you. This has to be our last time. We can't do this anymore."

He jerks up shocked at the news. Mia sits up as well anticipating him blowing up on her for dropping the bombshell. He finally screams out.

"MIA?!"

That's not Terry's voice. Mia covers her mouth and gasps.

"MIKE?!"

The hotel room lights suddenly turn on. Mike and Mia are facing each other. Mia screams as Mike jumps out of the bed. Mia covers her body and face with the bed sheet.

Mike is feeling a bunch of emotions at once as he paces back and forth on the opposite side of the room. He starts to say something then stops. He starts again then stops again. He's flustered and can't manage to string together a simple sentence. He curses out loud.

"You're cheating on me?"

Mia snatches the sheet from her face and looks at him with a "really" look on her face. She fires back.

"You're cheating on ME!"

Mike claps his hands as he replies.

"But you knew that already."

Mia scoffs, as if that is an acceptable reply to what she just said. The nerve of this man to really be upset right now when they've both been caught red handed.

Coming to the hotel today, Mia's biggest fear was Terry's reaction to her announcement but never in a million years could she have imagined the day would turn out this way. All this time Mia thought Mike was turning over a new leaf. He was home more, actively attentive to her and making love to her as if she was the only one. The biggest sign Mia used to think Mike had stopped cheating were the gifts stopped coming. But the entire time he's been sneaking off to a hotel to meet other women. She feels so stupid right now and even worse, she wasn't even with Terry.

Mike's face shows shock, betrayal and distraught.

"Me knowing doesn't make it right. You shouldn't be doing it in the first place."

"But you didn't seem to care." Mike says.

Mia leaps out of the bed walking over to him. She steps in front of him. Mia stands in front of him making him look at her.

"Of course I care! I just figured there was nothing I could do to stop you so," Mike interrupts her, "So you out here in these streets!?"

Mia knows she should feel bad at this moment but she's not going to allow Mike to gaslight her and deflect from the fact he's here as well. It's not like she walked in on him like she did. He had sex with her thinking it was someone else and she's not going to let him skirt around that fact.

"Oh don't try to make me out to be the bad guy. I was just following your lead."

Mike can't believe what he's hearing. She is the bad guy! She's cheating! How is she making this about him? She knew what he was doing, she's known since college.

"My lead?" He asks as he slides down the wall onto the floor wrapping his arms around his knees and rocking back and forth.

"Yes!" Mia exclaimed, "You started it!" Mike shoots back.

"YOU started it!"

Mia throws her hands up in the air and is now the one pacing around the room.

"How sway?"

Mike stammers his words, unable to get a clear sentence out.

"Exactly," Mia says. She furiously hits her phone, turning off the music.

Silence falls over the room. Mike and Mia calm down. They avoid eye contact and don't say a word to each other. Mia snatches the sheet off the bed and wraps it around her as she sits on the edge of it with her back to Mike and her arms folded. There were times where Mia feared Mike finding out about her infidelity. She wondered what that would mean for their marriage. Would he leave her? Or worse, in a fit of rage would he hurt her? She wondered if he was even capable of that. Mike isn't a violent man. Most people aren't violent but given the right situation and everyone can be capable of doing anything.

Mia thinks about what she should do next. She can understand Mike isn't in the best space right now to hear her explanation, he's still trying to process what's just unfolded. Now the dust is settling, Mia's maternal instincts kick in. She does feel bad about how Mike feels in this moment but she doesn't feel bad for her actions. She had to do what was best for her and despite the way she went about doing it, she doesn't regret it.

Mia knows why she did what she did. No it wasn't planned but Mike did push her in this direction whether he wants to admit it or not. The only thing Mia thinks about now is if she and Mike can move past this. She's always said she doesn't want to leave her marriage but it may not be up to her at this point.

If Mike does choose to leave her, a part of her will be hurt, naturally. But the other part of her is OK with that possibility.

Mike, on the other hand, is a complete mess right now. So many things flood his mind it's hard for him to focus on one singular thought. The thought that keeps resurfacing is the men in the barbershop were right. How did he miss the signs? Was he so wrapped up with his running around that he neglected to see Mia had begun to do the same?

He accepts no responsibility for Mia cheating. He's completely dismissed the fact that he is also cheating, he came here today to cheat and he thought he was cheating with Allison. But he doesn't think about that. He thinks about Mia being with another man and his ego is taking a huge hit. He wonders if this mystery man is better looking than him? Is his dick bigger? Does he have more money than he does? Did Mia let him shoot the club up or worse? Did she swallow? Did she take it in the face? Did the man do things he didn't know Mia liked? The images of what Mia potentially did with her sneaky link causes Mike to cringe at every thought.

He never thought the tables would turn on him. In one conversation Mike had with Clive he once said if Mia ever found out he would expect consequences but he never thought she would get him back like this. Her sleeping with another man was the furthest from his mind. His arrogance is really at fault here but that's not what he wants to hear right now.

After what seemed like hours, Mia gets up. She sits next to Mike and tries to touch him but he pulls away acting overly dramatic.

"Oh God no! Don't touch me, don't touch me! Go wash your hands, go wash your hands!" Mia looks at him confused.

"Wash my hands? Why?" Mike looks at her with all seriousness in his eyes as he replies.

"You can't touch me with the hands that touched another man. Oh God!" Mike gags.

Mia's now tired of Mike's antics. She jumps to her feet pacing around the room trying to explain herself. She decided to accept her part in this mess but she also wants to let Mike know exactly why.

"Baby I'm sorry. I made a huge mistake. But what else was I supposed to do? For the last six years I felt unwanted and neglected. Every time you came home with a gift I felt this pain in my heart because I knew what it meant. You have no idea what that feels like."

Mike's heart sinks. Damn, she knows what the gifts were for. He thought she would think they were mere tokens of his affection for her but he should have known she's a woman and women are smarter than that. Mia shattered his fragile world again by informing him he wasn't as slick as he thought he was. The gifts didn't throw Mia off, it confirmed what he was doing and she now knows just how many times he's done it. Instead of hearing Mia and accepting his part in pushing her into the arms of someone else, Mike claps back.

"Don't tell me I don't know what it feels like." Mia doesn't back down.

"I wanted to feel loved and desired and sexy. You weren't giving that to me. YOU LEFT ME ALONE ON MY BIRTHDAY!! What was I supposed to do?"

Mike looks up at Mia, a light bulb goes off in his head. He can't believe it.

"That's when it started?!" Mike asks.

Mia stops pacing and turns her back to Mike shaking her head. Mike jumps up and walks over to her pressing her for confirmation to his assumption.

"Oh don't get quiet now! Tell me the truth. You've been smashing niggas since your birthday?"

Mike gets in Mia's face. She pushes him away but he barely moves, he stays in her space demanding the answer. Mia thinks about grabbing her clothes and leaving the hotel room but she stays. Her mother used to tell her that no one changes anything until they get upset. Mike is upset right now and if Mia wants him to change his ways, she's going to have to tell him the brutal truth. If he leaves, he leaves. Maybe he'll remember how he feels in this moment and be better for the next person. If he stays, he has to know that his behavior needs to stop. Mia looks Mike square in the eyes.

"It isn't niggas. It was just one man!"

Mike gasps, his mouth gapes open, his eyes bug out. Mia sees his reaction but she does not waver. She stands firm, poised and confident. This is the moment of truth. There's no turning back now.

"You in a whole relationship with another nigga!" Mike pretends to faint and falls backwards on the bed. Mia's not amused. She actually feels kind of good to see Mike feel what she's been feeling all these years. She holds out both her hands.

"Would you rather it be with one dude or several dudes?"

Mike groans at the thought. He sits up on the bed shaking his head no. Silence falls between them again. Mike looks at Mia with fear in his eyes. He lowers his voice and talks softly, almost not wanting the next words to leave his lips in fear of the answer. He stutters, "Did- did, y-y-y you give him the gwak, gwak 3000?" Mike bites his fist, tears swell in his eyes. Mia rolls her eyes, doesn't answer.

"Mike."

Mike cuts her off. He doesn't want to hear anything except yes or no.

"No! Did you suck..." Mike gags, he tries to continue, "Did you give him head..." Mike gags again.

Mia takes a deep breath. She's over Mike acting childish so she blurts it out.

"YES! YES! I SUCKED HIS DICK!"

A housekeeper walking down the hallway hears what Mia said. She stops walking, looks at the room door, gets really close to it and yells, "That's right girl! Take his soul!"

Mike jumps up and runs to the bathroom. Mia follows but Mike closes the door and locks it in her face. He sticks his head in the toilet vomiting, talking and crying at the same time.

"Oh lawd, no, no, no, no. Not my baby."

Mia bangs on the door calling Mike's name repeatedly. "Mike! Mike! Com'on! You're overreacting!"

Mike lifts his head out of the toilet and turns to the door yelling.

"How many times? Every time?" Mia responds.

"I'm not answering."

"TELL ME!" he yells.

Mia exhales rolling her eyes as she continues banging on the door.

"You tell me, how many Mike?" Mike looks at the door wide eyed.

"Huh?" Mia hits the door out of anger.

"Nigga if you can huh you can hear. How many women your mouth been on?" Mike gets quiet.

Mia listens with her ear to the door. She hears the water running, then turn off. The door opens, Mia steps back. Mike looks at her with sad eyes.

"How many?" Mia looks at him matter of factly, folding her arms.

"Yeah! Stop stalling. It's been six years and I have a closet full of I'm sorry gifts so just tell me. How many?"

Mike looks around avoiding eye contact with Mia but she moves her head toward his eyes every time he moves. Mike looks at Mia, wincing.

"Total number or.... how many at once?" Mia's eyes widened.

"You had threesomes!"

Mike slightly ducks as he answers yes. Mia screams as she wildly punches Mike over and over as he tries to shield his head.

"You son of bih..."

Mike jukes out of the way and runs around the room while Mia chases him trying to inflict more hits. Mike grabs the chair from the desk and puts it between himself and Mia.

"What does it matter if it was a threesome or not?" Mia clams down.

"Cause! You never asked me for a threesome! But you out here with other women." Mike's eyebrows jump. "You'd have a threesome?"

Mia flops down on the bed rubbing her head.

"I don't know. Maybe. But we shoulda had a conversation about what you want, what you like and allow me to decide. But you never gave me that chance." Mike sits in the chair facing Mia.

"You right. I just assumed that wasn't you. And that's OK, I didn't want to pressure you or guilt you into doing anything. But I coulda asked."

Mike and Mia sit silent for a while. Then Mia asks, "So now what?" Mike exhales, shaking his head. He searches for the right thing to say. For the first time since the lights came on. Mike was in a state of shock. Now, knowing somewhat of the extent to Mia's cheating, Mike starts to think clearly.

As much as it pains Mike to know Mia's allowed another penis in her, reality sets in. He looks at Mia, his wife who's looking at him just as hurt and embarrassed as he is. He sees himself and Mia on the same level. They've both cheated, despite how or why or how many times, they've both done it. He now understands he's in no position to be as upset as he is. He also realizes that regardless of the countless times he's cheated on Mia, she hasn't left him.

He wants to be able to say he wants to end the marriage, however, Mike likes to think he lives by a code. It's a loose moral code but he listens to it in this moment. He looks at Mia, no anger. Tenderly and says, "I don't know. What would you like to do?"

Ready to answer and say stay married, something stops Mia faster than the words can come out.

Mia thinks Mike is looking for a way out. He's expecting her to tell him what she wants to do so he can answer accordingly. Mia knows this and she's not going to let him do that. They are both in the hotel room, naked and caught cheating. If Mike wasn't out in the streets doing God knows what with God knows who, they wouldn't be here right now. Mia decides the best thing to do is to put the ball where it belongs. In Mike's court.

"It's not about what I want to do. No matter what I say, you're going to do what you want to do. You always have. So let's decide right here and right now. How do you want to move forward? Together? Or apart?"

Mike doesn't look at Mia but can feel her eyes burning a hole in his face. Mike fidgets. His knees shake. Palms are sweaty. He hears his heart beating rapidly. Mike finally musters up the courage to be vulnerable and say what he wants.

"I want to stay married."

Mike swallows hard after letting it come out. Mia looks at him as she fights back tears. It's confirmation of what he whispered in her ear when he thought she was sleeping.

"Your turn."

Mia's always known what she wants. She's said it several times.

"I want to stay married. I want you Mike. I always have. And I want the opportunity to grow into the woman you want sexually."

Mike nods his head trying not to be overly happy with her answer. He thinks, then looks at Mia with a smirk on his face.

"Would you have sex with me and wear a power rangers costume?" Mia chuckles.

Mike eventually joins her when he realizes she's not laughing at him. He relaxes a little knowing Mia is providing a safe space for him to be honest about his sexual desires. "Sure baby." Mia says.

Mike walks over to Mia. He smiles at her and looks at her tenderly. He kisses her. The image of Mia with another man flashes through Mike's mind like Lance at the altar in the Best Man movie. He jerks back, stumbling into the TV, eyes wide like he's seen a ghost. Mia looks lost.

"What! What's wrong?" Mike trembles.

"I keep seeing you with another man. I can't get that thought outta my head."

Mia curses her lips and tilts her head to the side.

"Now imagine having those thoughts for six long years."

Mia's words smack Mike in the face. He heard her loud and clear. He softens, looks at Mia speaking in an honest tone. Mia feels the sincerity in his voice.

"I promise you. I will never touch another woman again." Mia smiles.

"And I will not touch another man again. The slate is clean. For the both of us."

Mia leans in for a kiss. Mike hesitates but he closes his eyes and the two kiss. Mike and Mia hug tightly, both with smiles on their faces. Mike and Mia spend the rest of the afternoon talking things out. They door dashed food and ate over having tough conversations. They didn't reveal the names of their lovers but spent the time explaining what they did for them.

Hearing all the things Mike did with so many women was tough for Mia to hear. But it wasn't as tough as Mike hearing about how Mia's lover saved her from misery. Mike had no idea his actions caused that kind of pain on Mia. Mike learned he was very naive in thinking she wasn't affected by his cheating. Mia wouldn't allow him to use the excuse that she stayed with him through it.

Mike came to the conclusion that he isn't the man for Mia, he thought he was. Just because she put up with his foolishness for so long doesn't make anything he was doing right. He had to ask himself and answer the hard questions Mia asked. If he knew Mia was the woman for him, why couldn't he be faithful? Why did he think he could go on for as long as he did without it coming to an abrupt end?

As the afternoon turned to evening, the rain has stopped but the sky is still gray. Mia and Mike's conversation has moved on from the tough topics and moved into the sex topic. Mike spoke the most. He opened up about the things he's experienced and the things he would like to do with Mia.

Surprisingly, Mia was down for a lot of it. But on the topic of threesomes, she hesitates. She explained to Mike that it's one thing knowing Mike is sleeping with other women. But it's a whole different ball game to watch him please another woman. Mike tries to spin it in a way that the experience could be beneficial to them both, however, Mia explains that she has no desire to interact with the other woman.

To put it in perspective for Mike, Mia asked him would he be open to having a threesome that involves another man pleasing her? Mike undoubtedly says no. His answer helps Mia's case. Mike counters with asking Mia if she actually wants to see him interact with another man sexually.

Of course Mia says no but Mike points out that's the difference between a two-woman threesome and a two-man threesome. But Mia challenges him back by saying, he doesn't have to interact with the other man. The other man is there for her pleasure. The two go back and forth on the subject before deciding to table it for a later time.

The couple decides to spend the night at the hotel. They both check their phones to see if their lovers contacted them when they didn't show up but neither Terry nor Allison has reached out. Mia figured they were probably doing the same thing she and Mike were doing, enjoying their time with each other.

For Mike and Mia, the butterflies are back for the both of them. They feel giddy and childish like they did in their first few months in college. It's almost as if their relationship did not end, it didn't start over but it's been revived and everything is new. Mia looks forward to the days, months, weeks and years to come.

For Mike, there's been a weight lifted off his shoulders now that Mia knows everything. He does fear he'll fall back into his old ways when and if the opportunity presents itself but he is determined to be better. Mia deserves it.

After what Mike and Mia were doing in the dark came to the light, they never contacted Allison and Terry again. The non-communication went both ways. Secretly Mike and Mia were on pins and needles expecting a fall out from them ghosting Allison and Terry. But after a few weeks the angst went away.

It was easier than Mia thought it would be to cut off Terry. She realized that she was just in her head all along. Mia couldn't wait to tell Denise what had happened at the hotel that day. Denise, although listening attentively, doesn't believe Mia when she told her Mike professed he'd be faithful.

"Once a dog, always a dog. But hey, if you wanna learn the hard way, by all means." She said as the two were locking up the salon for the night.

"I gotta have faith, right?"

Denise playfully swings the broom at Mia who ducks out of the way.

"Faith yes. But if this goes south, and it will, it'll be stupidity." Mia shakes her head no.

"That's not gonna happen."

"Cap! Denise shouts.

"It won't because he knows I can get it just as easy as he can and he's not gonna let that happen."

Denise thinks Mia may be on to something. Mia may think it's Mike's love for her that's bringing his ass home at night but Denise thinks it's pettiness. Regardless of what it is, they both are happy with the way things are going now.

"Sooooo, you gonna give me Terry's number?" Denise teases. Mia gives her a look.

"I'll kill you!" she threatens. Denise laughs.

"It's not like you're gonna be using it again."

The women walk out of the salon, Mia locks the door behind her. They stand in front of the salon looking up and down Peters street taking in the sights of the Atlanta art district. Cars ride slow down the tight two-lane street blasting music.

Patrons stand in a long line outside of the soul food restaurant Old Lady Gang. Other people walk in and out of other bars and restaurants that line the streets while the boot man keeps an eagle eye on parked cars. Mia takes everything in with a smile on her face. This is what happiness feels like. She has a successful business in a city that she loves and she shares a beautiful home with the love of her life. What more can she want?

Mia's so focused on being thankful for her life that she doesn't hear Denise calling her name. Denise nudges her, "Earth to Mia!" Denise waves her hand in front of Mia's face then snaps her fingers. Mia snaps out of it.

"Yeah. Uh?" Denise looks at her strangely but proceeds with repeating her question.

"Terry. The number. Lemme get it."

Mia laughs and walks toward her car without answering Denise. Denise follows her pleading for Terry's phone number. Mia opens the car door but Denise stops her. She looks at Mia with suspicion in her eyes. She waves her index finger in Mia's face.

"You ain't slick. You keepin' it for yourself, ain't you?" "What?" Mia asks in the most non-convincing way possible trying to hold back her laugh.

"Bish you heard me. You keepin' it for a rainy day dick." Mia looks at Denise confused.

"Rainy day dick?" Denise nods her head and pops her tongue, "Yep. Just in case Mike fuck up again."

Mia plays it off as she moves Denise out of the way and she gets into the car.

"I have no idea what you're talking about?"

"OK play dumb," Denise warns, "We'll see."

Mia goes to close the car door but not before she tells Denise goodnight. Denise replies, "Love me." Mia says, "Love me more."

They blow kisses to each other then Denise finally walks away from Mia's car.

Giddy, Mia drives home anticipating running into Mike's loving arms. Since the reveal she's moved all the gifts Mike had given her into their shared master closet. She can now enjoy them knowing that any gift Mike gives her will not be because of his guilt. They will be gifts from the heart, no string attached.

Mike and Mia promised not to keep any secrets between each other. That day in the hotel room they decided that they both would start off with a clean slate. They were not going to hold the past against one another. That day marked the first day of their new-ish marriage. They also mutually agreed not to tell each other the names of the individuals they had an affair with. However, Mia is keeping one secret from Mike. She hasn't shown Mike the closet full of gifts that she'd purchased during her time with Terry.

She wondered if she should give Mike the gifts or would the presence of them open the door they've already closed. Mike knows she started the affair with Terry on the night of her birthday but what he doesn't know is that it was a weekly affair and not a once in a blue moon type of relationship.

Things have been going so well with them both that Mia doesn't want to take two steps back after they've taken so many steps forward. She holds her breath every time Mike is upstairs alone or when he walks past the hallway closet. While Mia is trying to figure out what to do with the gifts, Mike is handling his new way of life pretty easily. The women haven't stopped throwing themselves at him whenever Mia's not on his side, however, he takes a lot of pride in saying I'm married. The first time he said it was the day after the hotel situation.

Mike was at a gas station putting the gas pump back on the handle when a homeless man asked for money. He'd given the man money which caught the attention of the woman at the pump adjacent to his. She watched the interaction and decided to strike up a conversation with Mike.

"I bet you're the type to put your grocery cart back too huh?" She said with a smile.

Mike looked at her but not the way he normally looks at women. He kept his eyes above the neck as he spoke with her.

"Don't you?" he asked. The woman whispers, "Not all the time but don't tell on me." They shared a laugh.

As Mike was getting into his car to leave, the woman scurried over to his driver side window and asked him if he knew she was flirting with him? Mike bashfully smiled then held up his ring finger.

"I'm married."

The woman nodded and looked away for a second, thinking of a snappy comeback.

"I didn't hear happy in that sentence." Mike slightly laughed.

"You're right. I'm happily married."

"Too bad," the woman said as she walked off.

She was absolutely a brick house but Mike didn't look at her butt when she walked away. Instead, he sat in the car chuckling to himself, enjoying the feeling of rejecting the woman who clearly wanted him.

He felt better than he did when he took a woman up on her advances. He never thought turning down someone so beautiful and forward would be so easy and feel so good. He was proud of himself and after that day, he never looked back. Since, he's turned down 18 women but who's counting?

The thought of Mia with another man is still difficult for Mike to get out of his head. The main thing he thought about was just how many times she'd been with him since the affair started. Remembering they both agreed to start anew, he's been reluctant to ask her. But everyday it gets more and more difficult not to ask.

In their clog foot tub, Mia lays between Mike's legs as he uses a loofah to wipe the soap off her shoulders. Mia enjoys the hot water cascading down her shoulders, back and chest. She rubs Mike's shins as she pushes both his legs tighter around her. She exhales pleasantly as she leans back into his chest.

Mike runs the loofah over her breasts focused on her nipples knowing it's one of her spots.

"Don't start nothin'," she warns as she closes her eyes.

Mike laughs but continues on the other breast. During a time Mike should be focusing on the gorgeous naked woman in front of him, he finds his thoughts are elsewhere. The question of how many times Mia had the affair pops up in his head again. He tries to shake it off to enjoy teasing Mia but he can't.

Suddenly, he asks.

"Hey, just how many times were you and that guy together."

Mia's taken aback. Her eyes fly open and she jerks up. Mike wasn't expecting that kind of physical response. But now that she's responded the way she has, Mike really wants to know how. Mia stutters searching for the right thing to say.

"Wh...why....why d..d...do you ask?" Mike shrugs. "Just wanted to know. You know how many times I cheated."

Mia grows uncomfortable not knowing how Mike would react to the truth.

"We decided to leave the past in the past, remember?" Mike replies, "Yeah I do but I can't shake this. I promise, if you tell me, we never have to talk about it again." Mike holds up his pinky finger.

Reluctantly and after a few moments of thought, Mia pinky swears with Mike. She turns around facing him. Mike tenses up in anticipation of the number. They both are nervous about the next words to leave Mia's lips.

"I can't tell you," she finally says. Mike looks upset but he doesn't show it in his tone.

"Ple-," Mia cuts him off.

"I'd rather show you."

Mia gets out of the tub. Mike sits there thinking how could she show him, he's beyond confused. He looks at Mia put on her bathrobe and slippers, then stands at the entrance of the bathroom door. She holds out her hand.

"You coming?"

Mike exits the tub wrapping a towel around the lower half of his body. He takes Mia's hand and she leads him out of the bathroom. She walks in a slow pace toward the linen closet, a knot in the pit of her stomach and everything in her mind screaming not to do it.

Mike attempts to figure out what Mia has to show him. Doubt sets in and he's not sure he even wants to know now. But it's too late. He's about to find the answer to the question that's plagued him the past few months.

Mia opens the linen closet door and stands in front of it. Mike looks but all he sees are towels and washcloths. Then Mia moves towels from several of the shelves revealing ten different gifts. Mike steps closer inside and he can't believe his eyes. He puts his hands on both sides of his face and screams, "NOOOOOOOOOOOOO!!!!"

<h1 style="text-align:center;font-style:italic;">Chapter 9</h1>

The next day, Mike lays on the floor in the fetal position rocking side to side. A distraught look on his face muttering to himself. Dr. Phil sits with his legs crossed, notepad on his lap as he watches Mike have what looks like a nervous breakdown. His shoes are mismatched and he's dressed as if a five-year-old dressed himself with the lights off.

Dr. Phil finally asks, "So Micheal. Is the issue that she had an affair or had an affair so many times with the same man? Because you did the same thing with Allison."

Mike stops rocking. He looks at Dr. Phil.

"No! The issue is she did it and bought a gift after every time. She pulled a me on ME! Don't you see, that's diabolical!"

Dr. Phil rolls his eyes, exhales, "Well Michael you did give her the blueprint." Mike sits up with his back on the bottom of the sofa.

"Yeah but ten times! How sway!? There were no signs! She didn't stay out late. She always came home. She didn't change up the way she looked like most women you see in the movies. All the textbook signs that a woman is having an affair, she didn't do. Her level of deception is unmatched by anything I did. Plus, she runs two salons. Where did she find the time?"

Mike thinks for a second then continues.

"I'm disturbed but also impressed. Then again I wonder if it's still going on or if she'd do it again."

Mike looks at Dr. Phil hoping he'd reassure him that Mia wouldn't cheat again. Unfortunately, they both know Dr. Phil can't make a promise like that. Instead, the good doctor says, "Well you know what they say Michael. Women do it best. Looks like you're gonna have to make some changes to ensure that doesn't happen again."

Mike thinks as he completely gets off the floor. He stares off into space while shaking his head.

"I don't think I'll ever be the same."

Dr. Phil uncrosses his legs. He sits up leaning over putting his hand on top of Mike's hand. Mike looks up at Dr. Phil like a lost little boy.

"Michael, you have to look at the bright side." Michael thinks.

"What bright side?" he asks. "The only bright side is I'm not playing step daddy to some other dude's child."

Dr. Phil shakes his head no.

"The bright side is you now have a great monogamous relationship with your wife. She didn't leave you."

"Yeah but she cheated, ten times!" Dr. Phil looks Mike square in the eyes.

"Sounds like cheating saved your marriage."

After Dr. Phil's words registered in Mike's head, all Mike could think about was choking Dr. Phil to death. Of course he didn't. The better course of action for Mike would be to take Dr. Phil's $400 an hour words and see them clearly. Dr. Phil is right, as Mike hates to admit it, Mia's cheating did save their marriage. Mike has to sit with the reality that he wasn't making Mia happy, in fact, he was doing more damage than he could have ever imagined. His actions could have destroyed a beautiful soul of a woman and left her broken for the next man to try to fix.

However, Mia's stronger than that and Mike knows it. If Mia didn't take it upon herself and put her happiness in her own hands, nothing would have changed. They would have never gotten into the same hotel room that day and they would have never addressed the elephants in the room. Mike would have never been able to truthfully express his desires without the fear of retribution and Mia would have never shown Mike she should do it better.

If none of that happened, Mike would've never turned down the woman at the gas station let alone the other 17 women. Part of being a better man, a better husband is also having the tough conversations with yourself. In addition, it means taking the advice from a professional, especially one you're paying.

Cheating did save their marriage. Mike knows that now. He never looked at it that way but he now knows it's true. So no longer will he focus on how many times Mia cheated, it doesn't matter. What matters is now, who cares how they got here. He's happy. His wife is happy and all is right in the world.

Mike finished his internal conversation unaware of how long he's been in his own head. When he comes back to reality he sees Dr. Phil is gone. Mike looks around calling Dr. Phil's name to no avail. He looks down at his lap to find a handwritten note that says, *Out for lunch, lock up*. Mike can't believe Dr. Phil left him there alone. He laughs.

Later that night Mia sits on the sofa in comfy clothes flicking through the TV looking for a movie to watch. She hears Mike in the kitchen, she calls to him.

"Babe! You want a drama or comedy?"

In the kitchen Mike spoons food on two plates from a pot he's holding. He's never cooked dinner for Mia before and is very proud of how his dish has turned out. He answers back.

"Let's do a comedy. We've had enough drama."

He hears Mia laughing in the living room, he laughs as well. Mike finishes plating the food. Wipes his hands then picks up both plates leaving the kitchen. He enters the living room with the food. He sets them down on the coffee table. Mia looks over the food smiling then she gives Mike a kiss.

"Aww thank you baby. It looks great for your first time." Mike flexes.

"What can I say? You married a talented dude."

They both share a laugh then sit back on the sofa. Mike picks up Mia's plate and feeds her the first bite. She closes her eyes savoring the flavor exploding on her taste buds. Mike anxiously asks, "Is it good?" Mia opens her eyes, swallowing.

"It's amazing.' Mike smiles.

"Just wanted to do something to show you I love and appreciate you."

Mia's heart melts then she remembers.

"Oh, I almost forgot."

Mia bends down looking under the sofa, Mike's confused as to what she's doing or what could be under the sofa. Seconds later, Mia pops back up with a wrapped gift in her hands. When Mike sees the gift he jumps to his feet knocking the plate of food on the floor. He runs around the house going from room to room screaming, "NOOOOOOOOOOOO!!!!!!"

ArLancia Williams

AUTHOR OF "CHEATING SAVED MY MARRIAGE."

ArLancia was born and raised in the Washington, DC region. She is a loving wife, a girl's mom of 3, a stepmom and a devoted care provider to her mom. ArLancia always dreamed of writing a book and recently decided to pursue her passion for writing while at her mom's bedside. It was then, she decided to write a funny novel about marriage and adulterers, hoping to send a message to married couples to marry the person you want, and not the person you hope they become after marriage. Secondly, you don't have to throw your marriage away after adultery–It can be fixed, but only if you really love each other.

Arlancia has many more ideas up her sleeve and "Cheating Saved my Marriage," is only the beginning of what she hopes to be a long successful career as a renown author.